The Lady of the Tower

by
Gwen Dandridge

The Lady in the Tower is a work of fiction. Names, characters, places, and incidents are either the product of the author's imagination or are used fictitiously. Any resemblance actual persons, living or dead, is entirely coincidental.

Published in the United States by Hickory Tree Publishing.

ISBN: 978-1-7334091-9-3

Cover Illustration @ Laura-Susan Thomas
Book Design by Angela Borda

Dedicated to
My sister-friend, Susan Rush Rouch, a true celebrator of
life with all its ups and downs.

Part I
The
Tower

Prologue

From within the mirror, the guardian watched in helpless horror. Six times it had happened, six girls and then six lads drawn up into the Tower and locked pair by pair within one of seven panels gracing the wall. And, powerful magician though he had been, his efforts had not made the least difference.

This sixth time, he didn't call out for Roselyn to stop. It would change nothing; his daughter couldn't hear him anymore. Or if she did, she didn't respond. His child, whom he loved beyond all things, slept in restless distress. But in her sleep, she entangled others into her magic, dooming them to a half-life within the walls of the Tower.

All he could do was despair and try to ease the young couple's final days. His gaze shifted from the current lovers fighting the wall's pull to stare again at the seventh panel, the only one remaining empty. If the past six were any indication, the last girl would arrive within days. And a month or so later, the final boy.

He winced as this sixth girl, Dulce, the boy had named her, met his eyes in a desperate plea. He turned his head, unable to bear the scene before him. The lad's arms wrapped about Dulce as though he could defend against the inevitable. No hope existed; Roselyn's magic was powerful, and she listened to no one.

The guardian drifted back within the mirror's depth. He couldn't help. All that remained for him was a handful of pitiful spells, only enough to give the trapped some comfort.

He bowed his head. The end neared, for him, for those trapped, and for his daughter. One last time, the final panel would fill and then…

Chapter

1

Light trickled across my eyelids. My dreams had been disturbing, dark, and unsettled. I lay in bed, eyes closed, as I tried to remember what was causing my unease, but it skittered across my mind, leaving a distressing blank. I heard the *tit-tit-tit-tswee-tswee* of a chiffchaff warbler outside saluting the morn and then, far in the distance, the *kee-kee-kee* of a kestrel.

Something soft drifted across my face, tickling my nose and cheeks.

I blinked open one eye and then the other. Above me, rose-colored bed-curtains wisped across my face. High above that, twenty feet or more, a curved ceiling spanned the room; hand-carved joists divided it into eight sections shaped like a bramble rose.

Pushing down a film of fear poised to spill into my mind, I turned my head toward the light. A small linen-covered table and a single chair sat afore two many-paned doors. My eyes caught the wingtip of a swallow as it dashed past the opening to sit for half an eye's blink on the wrought-iron balcony. Steam from a silver teapot married with the intoxicating scent of cinnamon pastry.

I raised myself upon my elbows, trying to slow the rapid intake of my breath. Outside the doors, the land fell away. A few tall pines stretched up to the sky before the countryside rolled out into a shrubby glen that moved into woodland. Beyond that, purple mountain tops ascended to meet the horizon. It was bonny, if you liked that kind of thing.

Did I like that kind of thing? I scanned my memory.

Then tried again. Nothing.

My life was bare, stripped like a bed to its ticking.

My world before waking today—nothing. I could not even recall my name. My breath caught, fluttering like a grouse trapped in a net. I rolled to the edge of the bed. A tinned mirror, twice my height and as wide as a wardrobe, flanked the far wall facing the bed.

I inched toward the overcarved frame, terrified of what I would see.

A lass, her hair brushed and plaited into two braids of burnished sable, coiled neatly at the nape of her—er, my—neck, stared back. I pressed my hands to my mouth and then, self-consciously, moved them down my pink and buttercup silk gown, watching as the mirror reflected my motions. I stood there, staring at this stranger's face, her delicate arched brows over startled blue eyes, a full mouth, and a strong chin. I tried to get my bearings, tried to remember if I had ever looked like this, worn something like this afore.

And my name. What *was* my name?

I peered in the mirror again. The clothes I wore would not hold up against any kind of hard work. And, surely, I wouldn't have willingly woven so many pastel-colored ribbons through my hair. I thought again. Maybe I had liked that at some point. It seemed unlikely.

As I watched, the mirror glazed, and the glass fogged, swirling slowly, violet smoke churning deep within. As a shadowy face emerged, I whirled around, but no one was there. I spun back to face the mirror.

"May I assist you, my Lady?" A voice from within the mirror asked, as if it were cloaked by water.

I jumped back, tripping over the bottom of my fine silk nightgown. My eyes narrowed. Who was this intruder? "I'm nae your Lady," I snapped as I regained my balance. "I dinnae even think I am a Lady." But I re-examined the finery that flowed from my shoulders to my feet. Perhaps I was.

A shadowed face stared back at me: large, hooded eyes, a mouth, too tight—almost hidden beneath trimmed gray facial hair.

"Who are ye?" I asked, taking yet another step away from the mirror. "Actually, nae. Who am I?"

Disdain curled his lips. "You are the Lady of the Tower."

I reassessed my surroundings. I was in a tower. "Nae! You misunderstand. What is my name, not where am I."

"There is no difference," the voice insisted.

My fears grew by the minute. "What does that mean?" This wasn't right. None of this was familiar, not him, not this room, not even me. My gaze bounced across the different surfaces in the Tower: the elaborate murals on each wall, the crystal sconces holding tall ivory-colored candles. All spoke of riches, lots of it. This didn't feel natural. I would have remembered this much luxury. Too much. This screamed of magic. And 'twas a known fact, magic extracted a price.

"You belong to the Tower. She has claimed you."

I clamped my mouth shut and plopped down on my bum, suddenly overwhelmed. Some remote corner of my mind recalled stories of a cursed and enchanted tower, but not anything in particular. A whisper of a tinker's sister or the grandniece of a farmer or a distant cousin of a noble who had disappeared. Even remembering that much made my head ache.

I searched for a door, a staircase leading out, but saw nothing except the balcony with its picture-perfect view and the long, long drop to the earth.

The face in the mirror watched me. "There is no way out of here."

I bit my tongue, attempting to hold my peace, though to no avail as my questions spilled out.

"But why am I here? And why cannae I remember my past, nae even my name?" I insisted. Surely, once he said it, I would remember. "Have I been ill? Did I fall and bang my head?"

"Now that you belong to the Tower, your previous name exists no longer. It is lost and unimportant," he responded with a curt turn of his head. "The Tower removes memories of kith and kin as a kindness. You don't have a past. It is no longer relevant."

I swept my eyes across the room. All I saw was froth, from the plush patterned carpets covering the floor to the delicate pink of the segmented walls, each section painted with elaborate scenes.

"'Tis my life you are speaking of. Nae some kingdom's secrets." I pointedly glanced around. "There is nae else here but me—and ye, whoever ye are." I gathered my courage, edging closer to the mirror. Fog shrouded his face. Large feathered moths flapped wildly in my gut.

"You may call me *Guardian*. The Guardian of the Tower." His face glowed.

Against all reason, I laughed. "Some Guardian. Ye are stuck in a mirror."

His gaze glided over me again. "She shouldn't have selected someone from your station. You're not at all the proper kind of female to grace the Tower—no decorum, no sense of propriety. You don't speak the King's English. There was even dirt beneath your fingernails when you arrived."

I shot a quick glance at my roughened hands. "But...?"

"No more questions." The mirror clouded as he faded back

into its depths.

"Nae, wait, dinnae leave." But he did.

I stepped back from the mirror and peered at myself again. Surely, something about my looks would trigger a memory. My face appeared drawn, wide worried eyes in honey-colored skin. Was that color from the sun or breeding? I lifted my gown up to my thigh. My skin there was pale and white, unlike the tanned skin of my forearms. I was accustomed to being out in sunlight until recently. I held up my hands; my fingernails were short and tidied. No dirt remained from my past life, but calluses donned the tips of my left-hand fingers.

Before I had time to reconsider, I untied the laces and stripped off the gown, stomping it beneath my feet. I looked again. Even the small clothes were lace-covered. And pink, pink again. I turned my body sideways to the mirror and then swung forward. I was slender. Fairly modest on top with no breasts worth binding, a tiny waist and—I faced away, peering over my shoulder—rounded hips. There were muscles in my arms, and here and there a bruise bloomed on my skin. My left forearm sported a series of partially healed scratches running across it.

This was not the soft body of a noble. While I watched, the mirror glowed, and the guardian reappeared.

Shock crossed his countenance before he erupted. "Have you no modesty?"

A bevy of snaps and the clatter of wooden bells sounded from deep within the mirror, and the Tower walls misted. My neck hairs stood at attention. Ghostlike wraiths oozed from each of the murals adorning the walls. They pooled on the floor before rising and moving toward me. My breath caught in my throat. They floated across the floor, hovering over my trodden dress as I backed farther and farther away. The clatter from the mirror snapped again, and they solidified, listed toward me, dragging the gown with their limp white fingers. I made a futile attempt to run, circling the room once until I returned to where I started.

The wraiths edged toward me, closing in tighter and tighter to where I stood trembling like a coney beneath a kiting falcon. There was no escaping their hot, damp fingers pressing against my flesh. Accidentally, I looked into their milky eyes, and immediately I was lost in deep pools of sorrow and despair. My breath came in deep shuddering gulps as they pulled the gown over my head and laced before I could have whistled the first measures of an eight-bar reel.

Chapter

2

After banging on the walls and scrambling about the Tower, seeking an escape, I collapsed. My screams and shouts had brought no one. Throughout the rest of that day and well on into the night, I huddled against the side of the huge, fancy bed. My arms wrapped around my legs. I missed my… surely there was someone I missed or someone who missed me: a mother, father, siblings? I pressed my hands against my forehead, trying to recall any piece of my life. Perhaps I had a sweetheart, someone who loved me.

The night crawled on forever, stars creeping like snails across the sky. I must have dozed some as I opened my sleep-encrusted eyes to the sun peeking over the horizon. I sniffled, wiping my nose on the tail-end of my silk nightgown.

"Cease." He was back. "Have you no manners whatsoever?" his voice reproached.

The clang of bells sounded again, and the wall misted. The wraiths oozed forth once more. My breath caught in my throat and my teeth chattered as they drifted across the rich carpets. At a huge armoire, they hesitated, opened the cabinet doors, and removed a ruffled silk skirt and beribboned bodice in cherry blossom pink. I inched back, breath coming in deep gasps, suspecting what would come next. I counted six of them, though they seemed to merge into wispy clouds that pooled about each spectral figure.

"Just accept." And then he disappeared from view. I was too distracted to respond. They left the armoire and floated closer. I broke out in a sweat, trying to curl inward. Then they pressed against me, touching me. Heat pulsed from their hands as they removed my nightgown and clothed me in the new outfit. I heard a whisper, a word formed on the exhalation of a single breath. My mind slammed shut.

***

When my eyes opened again, the first thing I noticed was the self-proclaimed Guardian of the Tower. My gaze met his, and I lost our staring contest.

"Your breakfast is waiting," he said, pointing a white hand toward the linen-covered table. "If you continue to wallow in discontent, your food will grow cold. The youth attempting your rescue should have a comely lady to inhabit his dreams. Not some wiry scrap of a half-grown girl."

Wait, what was this? I understood then. "This is just a game, isn't it?" I sneered. "A wee distraction for the rich and bored."

He averted his gaze then, hiding some emotion. I watched, trying to read him. He continued as if I hadn't spoken, tsking, looking me up and down. "There's so much that could be improved: your language, your hair, your carriage. Well, nothing started, nothing gained."

My fear vanished as my temper rose. I turned my back on him and the food, but my nose twitched as the scent of a pastry reached me. I was hungry. A full stomach never hurt. I edged up from the floor and sidled over to the tray. My nose dripped again, and I hesitated as I prepared to use my—I glanced down—er, a Lady's morning dress, to wipe it. This dress was dove gray with rose-colored peonies embroidered across the hem. I reconsidered and ran the back of my hand across my nose. Behind me, he made a derisive noise.

When was the last time I ate? Certainly not yesterday. I picked up a small tartlet and bit down. Ahh. Warm apricot jam leaked out one side. I slurped it up quickly before it could fall.

"Use your napkin," his voice corrected. "Surely, you have basic table manners." I ignored him.

A silver teapot rattled gently to get my attention. I approached it carefully, opened its lid and sniffed—peppermint. I lifted the pot and poured myself a cup. When I lifted my gaze, I saw him squinting toward me into the brightness of the morning sun shoving through the double doors.

"Just because you were raised poorly is no reason to indulge your unladylike behavior. As the Tower's choice, you will learn to be well-mannered and tidy."

He was quiet for one peaceful moment. Then he started up again.

"It would help if you sat up and didn't hunch over the table like some cathedral gargoyle."

My eyebrows came down in a scowl.

"Don't ignore me! The *others* will return if you don't listen."

I heard him. I couldn't help but throw a fearful glance toward the walls. I skootched myself back in the chair, making some attempt at compliance.

He sniffed before prattling on. "That's better. During your time here, you will be properly dressed, coiffed, and mannered as befits the Tower. As I said, eventually, a man will come. They always follow after a Lady appears." He was silent, an expression of anguish crossed his face.

He seemed thoughtful. "They come in the name of love. This is the lull before they hear the Tower's call. It can take some time before your champion makes his way here. While waiting, you may spend your time embroidering and tatting."

"I dinnae dae fancy work." I took another bite of the apricot pastry, trying to block out his droning nasal voice. I glanced around once more. There was no way I would be here long enough for that to happen. I'd be out before the crows came down to nest.

He dismissed my comment with an annoying lift of his chin. "You don't remember. You can't. You must have done fine handwork at some point. You can't be *that* unnatural a female." He shook his head and closed his eyes as if disgusted. "You *could* merely sit, waiting, but the others all became despondent without some task." After a moment, he added, "And it's bad for your color."

"What happened to the others?"

He turned his face away.

"Fine, if ye won't tell me, then leave me be." I chewed with more enthusiasm, stuffing a second pastry in my mouth.

I could see him regarding me from his post at the mirror, and I clenched my teeth over the fruit tartlet. Two tears rolled down my chin before I could stop them.

"Now, now, I'm only trying to help."

I snorted.

He waved a disembodied hand over to the left. "There are tapestries over there. I'm sure there are a few unfinished that would be of interest."

I refused to speak, crunching down on the last mouthful of food. I scanned the room, seeking for the way out again. There had to be one. My eyes flicked over to the Guardian watching me.

He shook his head. "There is no escape from here."

I balled my hands in my lap. Maybe, but the others were gone. I would leave here also… and soon.

He continued, unable to shut his gob. "This moping is

unattractive. How about tatting? There is also a harp and a few other instruments that you can play if you are so inclined."

I could feel saliva welling up in my mouth.

"It isn't as if I am unfeeling. I want your time here to be pleasant. Enjoy our comforts."

I tapped my fork rapidly against the table in my irritation.

He tilted his head to one side. "Accept what has occurred. Sulking won't change anything." He swept his eyes across me again, assessing. "Though you lack the genteel demeanor of the others"— he nodded to himself—"that can be addressed."

Before I could think, I spat at him, splattering the mirror with a gob of spit. It was well aimed. Obviously, I had some experience with this, as I hit the mirror dead center. The mirror darkened, and the Guardian turned a bright, rowan berry red. Any pretense of agreeability was gone from his face. The bells clambered again, louder and more insistent. This time I did sprint around and around the Tower while the wraiths waited patiently, tirelessly, for me to weary. At last, I collapsed against a wall, breathing in deep gasps. They moved toward me, leaning in against me, suffocating me with their need and misery.

Just before I passed out, I heard a lass's voice say, "*Resist.*"

Chapter

3

As the days dragged by, I walked the perimeter of my Tower room over and over like a feral cat, searching for a breach in its defenses, some way out. I hefted carpets, looking for trapdoors; leaned out over the balcony to the long, long drop below; pressed my fingers along each stone, hunting for a crack, a lever—anything that might hide a doorway or a stair.

The Guardian watched, shaking his head. "Truly, child, you are wasting your time."

I snorted. He was trying to discourage me. People didn't build towers without creating a way in, and if 'twas a way in—'twas a way out!

"'Tis here. 'Tis merely a puzzle." I smirked, pleased to have figured this out.

I stopped in my tracks, thinking of the lassies held here before me. "Did the others try to escape, or did they sit primly with their hands politely clasped in their laps? Did ye watch them and laugh?"

There was silence from within the mirror.

I narrowed my eyes. "So, what finally happened? Were they rescued, or did they leave on their own?"

Some emotion flared in his face, but it was gone before I could identify it.

"No one has ever escaped. It is not possible."

"But ye said a champion comes, and they're nae here." I spun around, indicating the empty room. "They had to leave."

"She lets none of us..." His eyes winced in pain as he faded from my view, disappearing into the depths of his mirror.

I stood watching for some time, puzzling over his words before continuing my search.

No one was here, yet there had been lassies before me. If they hadn't escaped, where had they gone? I backed slowly away from the mirror, unable to bear where my mind was leaning. I shuttled those thoughts away and redoubled my search.

The Tower had windows, dark and dusty, facing three directions with heavy drapes hanging from high brass rods. Southward, a road curved past a derelict mansion, about two stones' throw away. Swallows dipped and dove through the mansion's broken windows, pigeons roosted in the eaves, and red squirrels scurried in and out through the open doors. Beyond that, the road meandered through brambly fields and heath-covered hills before disappearing into a forest.

I paced back and forth between the panels. All had murals painted in soft pastels. From my balcony, they appeared like happy pastoral scenes of a lass and lad. Different couples graced every one of the six panels. But on closer examination, the murals showed a fearful thing. In one, the tall reeds in a countryside pond had eyes. In the next, taloned hands reached out from an ancient sycamore and grasped the ankles of one couple. Within each panel, something lurked, and the happy smiles of the couple were offset by the despair in their eyes. I cringed whenever my gaze lit upon them.

One section sat empty. A blank easel. It drew me like a duck to a pond. Each time, my gut got a queasy feeling, and I quickly glanced away.

***

Within a few days, the Guardian and I had settled into a bitter struggle, like decades old sparring neighbors. Neither of us willing to let the other have the last word.

The longer I stayed a prisoner, the more frantic I became to leave, pacing and checking over and over each floorboard and wall for a hidden latch, something that would allow me to escape.

My temper rose when I didnae find it.

Once, I threw the teapot at the Guardian. It slammed against his mirror with a bang and bounced off, but the mirror didn't break. Not a crack. The Guardian was displeased with me that day. Quivering with anger through the tea-splashed mirror, he hissed a command. The bells clanged and bonged. I curled into a ball, bracing for the onslaught. And they came, placing their hands on my back, running their fingers through my hair. Every time I was sure that I could stand their presence, and each time I succumbed to their misery.

Increasingly, I listened for the voice—her voice. The wraith who spoke when they came. I could sometimes hear her in the few moments before I gave under the weight of their collective melancholy. A word or a phrase of encouragement would pass into my body along with the fear, and I drew strength from that to hope.

I knew every inch of my quarters now. The Tower was large, fifteen paces wide, about fifty steps around the inside of the room. A small balcony allowed me the only break beyond the confines of the stone walls.

Mornings, I would remove my gown and, dressed in my

23

knickers and chemise, I trotted around to clear my head of the lethargy after a night's sleep. It was enough to bring up a sweat after forty or fifty laps. The Guardian watched in disgust. That made the experience even better.

We fought over everything. When he wasn't watching me, I took my anger out on the Tower. With the dull butter knife that came with meals, I carved notches into the bedpost to mark my time. It felt satisfying, a way of keeping track. And something to prove a point.

I even thought to carve through the wall. But when I dug in the knife, I thought I heard soft weeping, and it put me off. It was to no avail, anyway; the walls healed as quickly as I carved a line.

Once I scratched the blank wall panel and felt a twinge of pain. A small scrape appeared across my arm, blood welling in tiny droplets. I stared for many heartbeats before backing away. For some days after, I couldn't bear to look at that panel. But I checked the healing scab on my arm often.

My only refuge was the balcony. There, I could sit and almost believe I was free. My hair unraveled from its braids and whipped around my head. I breathed in the fresh, cool air and gazed wistfully at the long drop to the earth. Seven stories high, too far to survive. I would end up splattered on the ground as raven pickings. I chewed my lip as I looked at the ground, contemplating the distance. It was so far. Some memory lightning-streaked across my mind, and I glimpsed myself scrambling up a sheer cliff.

I shivered. I'd climbed before, but when and how? If I had gone up something this tall, I could go down.

If I had but a rope, I could tackle this.

Chapter

4

A huge copper vat filled with steaming liquid appeared in the center of the room. I circled it, chewing at my cheek. The hairs on my nape stood upright, like a fox before a snare laced with poisoned bait. Finally, my curiosity overcame my resistance to speaking to the Guardian. "What's that for? Are ye going to dye wool?"

The Guardian leaned forward in the mirror. "Don't be obtuse. It's for you—you are filthy."

A tri-fold screen magicked between me and the mirror as those miserable bells clacked. I twitched in response. What had I done this time?

"Even you might desire some privacy during your bath."

I had washed my hands just that morning. Face, too. He faded back, leaving me wary, standing balanced squarely, prepared for anything.

My head swiveled from the mirror to the deep vat of water, to the wraiths folding out of the walls. There was no way they could be planning to put me in that hot water. My eyes narrowed as they circled me, herding me like spaniel dogs flushing grouse. Two edged closer. I swung my fist and felt them give way as if they were made of clotted cream.

'Twasn't a square go. All six of the wraiths surrounded me. I could make out faces now. Lassies, all. White skins and hair prissily coiled at their napes. And young, all of them young. The images from the wall panels.

A voice crept beneath my fear and anger. "*Gentle, gentle.*"

I couldn't tell if she was speaking to me or the other wraiths. I was beyond caring.

I fought as the wraiths dragged me to the tub, swinging arms and legs to no avail. I hollered as they stripped off my clothes and screamed as I was lifted bare-bum naked into the vat and screamed again as the perfumed water rose to my shoulders. I kicked and bucked. Water exploded every which way.

As the soothing warmth flowed around my body, I stopped. 'Twas lovely. I locked my fingers on the copper rim as they poured water over my hair and soaped it with sweet smelling suds.

Floating in the air, a wraith, her heart-shaped face, leaned in toward me. "*You must escape,*" she exhaled.

My heart beat out a triplet rhythm. "Who are ye?" My eyes crisscrossed looking at her translucent figure.

She pressed nearer, lips close to my ear. "*I'm Dulce. Please, please, leave this place.*"

"How? Tell me how," I mouthed back, wondering who we were trying to keep from hearing this conversation.

"*You're strong and clever. You must escape. Find my brothers—tell them…*"

The bells clanged again, and a mist wrapped around her.

"*Escape. Find the magic, and then return and release us!*" And she disappeared back into the wall.

Chapter

5

I retreated to my balcony, clean as a spring morning, recalling Dulce's words. I stared out in the distance, humming a bouncy hornpipe and watching the raptors ride the winds. Wishing I could fly away as well. But I couldn't, couldn't rescue myself, much less the wraiths. I turned over Dulce's plea. What magic could I get? I had none. I leaned over the edge of the balcony once more. The wall was sheer, cut from slick-faced stone, no nooks for a finger hold or place to jam in a toe. My lips twisted in frustration; it was way too far down. But again, I felt a fleeting something telling me I could do this, that once upon a time I had done something similar.

Nevertheless—there was magic to contend with; even out on this open-air balcony, I felt a pull to return within the Tower walls. Each time I pushed outside, I braced against a fear that beset me. But I stayed willing to bear it, to be beneath the sun washing across the sky. Within no time, my breath would ease. At night, I found myself drawn back inside to sleep in the overly soft bed. But with the next rise of the sun, I started yet again, struggling outside against forces I couldn't identify.

Below, I heard the raucous caw of ravens, miserable carrion birds, arguing over some scrap of food. Those black-feathered scavengers, never brave enough to travel alone, but gathered in clumps like village thugs. I wished for a pile of stones to throw.

Off to my right and down the hill, a flock of doves flew in and out of a window of the empty mansion. Long abandoned, I guessed, from the steady stream of birds winging through on their daily forages.

A lark trilled, and I added my whistle to its song, playing riffs off the melody. An arm's distance from me, a large orb spider sitting on the railing spun out a line and launched itself into the wind. He floated for a long moment, dancing in the air, before a wisp of wind turned him toward the Tower. He seemed to sense danger even before landing, twisting away, running back up the thin silver strand away from the stone wall. But it was too late. A breeze picked up, driving him back to the Tower.

He touched the wall.

There was a frenzy of activity, all eight legs flailing, before, in exhaustion, he stopped. Then it happened. A leg straightened; the now frantic creature struggled anew. I watched, in growing horror, as each segmented leg disappeared and he was drawn into the wall, slowly absorbed until he was gone.

A small black splotch, like the mark of a tinsmith, remained.

As I stared, the walls changed, swirling and clearing until I could see deep within. There, inside the yard-wide walls, a woman spun, her eyes shut, hair golden. She turned in her sleep, and from her fingers, thousands of strands sprang out. As she slept, she pulled, ever pulling, folding in those threads beneath restless hands, gathering to her anything she touched.

Surely, this could not be so. Not possible. Even as I saw it, I rejected it.

But, more and more, I sensed the Tower weaving a web of lethargy around me. My skin responded. I was no delicate noble to wilt before this, nor would I take the lure. I gritted my teeth. I now believed, nae, I knew, conceding this battle was death. I struggled, trying to recall a piece, a person, another memory; my head ached after.

No escape seemed possible. My dreams turned into nightmares where I eagerly caught a thread of her web and wrapped it about me as a shawl.

Below me in the glen, spring burst out. The woodland was covered with that particular shade of dusty violet before leaves break open from their buds. Wildflowers in red, white, and sun-yellow scattered across my view. My fingers slid from the edge of the balcony, and I curled into a ball. The only image in my mind was the empty panel.

Evening came, and my fingers turned blue from the chill air. I blew on them to ward away the cold, to give me a few minutes more. Only when I shivered uncontrollably did I creep back into the Tower, disgusted at another day in which I remained a prisoner.

Nothing entered the Tower, not a mouse, nor even a weevil—only me. After watching the spider, I knew why.

Early the next morning, after eleven days here according to my notched bedpost, I awoke to the light dusting of pollen blown from across the meadow. Spring continued to push in, and birds scrambled for the choicest nesting spots.

Given the number of raptors I saw, there must be a multitude of coneys hidden in the brush, but I was too far removed to observe them.

A vixen's bark carried up to me. I leaned over the ornate metal railing, trying to spy a tail or pricked ears peeking out from some thicket hidey hole.

The raptors commanded these skies: eagles, hawks, merlins, and peregrines, the queen of raptors. I followed the flight of a red kite and was quite pleased with myself to spy his aerie. There were other birds: geese, ducks, pipits, and blue martins, a pair of black storks winging toward the mountains. But the raptors grabbed my attention.

And always there were ravens, waiting, skulking, their ugly black heads pushed forward. Scavengers who built haphazard nests and watched for a careless raptor or a nest undefended. Bird killers.

A golden eagle shot down, striking the ground hard before he flew upward clutching a hare. I admired his strength and power, skill, and precision of his attack. Most of all, I envied his freedom. He could fly away.

While I watched, three ravens bothered themselves to lift up to the sky, wheeling after him the way they do, harrying him across the plains. Too lazy to get their own food, they thought to take his. Diving and dipping in with outstretched claws, each tried pushing the eagle enough to drop his prey, but never too close. Not near those razor talons. I leaned forward, my fingers wrapped around the balcony railing, unable to look away, willing the eagle to outrun these black feathered thieves. One particularly daring raven launched an attack, skimming the back of the eagle with his outstretched claws. The eagle twisted in pain, mid-flap, and his prey tumbled out of his grasp. The ravens watched it drop with avaricious eyes. The disgruntled eagle soared upward, glaring down at his tormenters. I nodded to myself. He'd make those ravens pay for that loss.

***

I dug my knife in the bedpost again, scoring the last cut; seventeen notches now, eight baths. May Day must not be far, as the days grew warmer, the sun lingering longer each night.

The Guardian and I had a wary peace now. I hadn't changed. Oh, perhaps I used a napkin more, but only because it was there. Handkerchiefs were simply gentler on my nose. Not because of him.

It was around then that I noticed minor disturbances out on the balcony. Small shiny items were missing. Even before I pushed the table back inside, I had my suspicions.

The next morning after my meal, I stood watch over my balcony table to see if something disappeared. Naught. I stepped back inside to grab my handkerchief, for a moment only, no longer than ten breaths. When I returned, the tiny silver jam spoon with its embossed pattern of swans was missing. Not that I cared about something so fancy, but I wondered what had taken it.

The next day, a pewter napkin ring disappeared, but this time a telltale clue lay beside my table, a black feather.

Ravens.

Chapter

6

Early the next morning, the Guardian watched me set up snares. "What is it about the ravens that has you so determined?"

"I hate them." I frowned, unable to recall the particulars. I finally settled on an answer. "They're vermin, and I want them gone."

"That's fairly obvious. But why? Why ravens? Why not wrens or swallows or chaffinch?"

He rested his chin on an armless fist as if in thought.

I pulled myself back from my newest snare. "Everyone hates ravens. How could ye not?"

Ignoring his curious stare, I returned to my work.

***

The following day was gray and overcast. After nineteen days, my restlessness was beyond containment. I explored the room again, rummaging through the embroidery and musical instruments, looking for bits and pieces to make a snare. Searching high and low for the way out, that elusive doorway I could feel tingling in my fingers. I lingered over the flute and then the harp until my hands rested on the fiddle. Nicely made. On the right corner of the upper bout, two initials were engraved: NP. Something twitched inside my head and then was gone. I turned the fiddle back over and plucked the strings. It needed tuning, but the wood was sound and well cared for. I twisted the tuning pegs of the first string, then fussed with the fine tuners until it sang a clear G.

The Guardian injected his unasked-for opinion. "A musician, how wonderful. I love the etudes and airs of violin."

I plucked another string and tightened it, comparing it to the first, then continued on to tune the other three strings until they hummed in harmony. My fingers itched to play. I ran my fingers across, playing scales, testing the action. Beautiful.

The Guardian leaned forward in his mirror. "I'm pleased. Not one of the previous ladies played the violin. It was just wasting away."

I rosined the bow slowly, wondering how long it had been since it was used. "How is it that my fingers know this if my memory has been erased?" I challenged. Not that I was softening toward him, not really. He was my only companion. 'Twas better than talking to myself.

"You don't forget how to walk or speak. Some behaviors transcend your everyday memories. Those stay. One girl even remembered the name of her dog."

"Where is she now, that girl?"

He remained silent.

I drew the bow across the fiddle. Almost; one twist more. I turned the screw on the bow and tested the tightness. It felt wonderful. I drew the bow across again, and the clear bell tones of a finely made instrument filled the room.

The Guardian leaned back as if awaiting a show, for some

court troubadour to play. I gazed far away out the window and played a lively country jig, my fingers sure. I knew I had spent many years doing this. The sounds bounced off the walls, and I played faster and boldly. The Guardian's brows drew down into a frown. Good, I thought. I switched to a bouncy reel and then a melancholy strathspey spilled out from my hands. Louder and surer, my fingertips moving back and forth with ease. My mind filled with a calm I hadn't felt since I arrived.

I watched the Guardian's face go from delighted to sour to panic as he listened.

"Stop, stop! Where did you learn that tune?"

I continued, pleased with the alarm that stuck on his face like an egg.

A tension shimmered through the walls. The Guardian must have felt it, too. A feeling that every stone was listening. "You're distressing her, hurting her."

I played faster and faster until my fingers ached and trembled with exhaustion. The walls of the Tower rippled. I gulped but pressed on with the tune. Within the wall's depths, a sound came. A female voice singing repeatedly:

Rose, Rose, Rose, Rose.
Will I ever see thee wed?
I will marry at thy will, sire,
at thy will.

"No, stop. Leave her in peace!" the Guardian screeched, the white tips of his fingers pressing against his mirror. The bells clanged, and the wraiths seemed tossed out of the walls, spinning and reaching as if pleading with me. In the interest of my sanity, I placed the fiddle down and backed out onto the balcony, watching in fascination as the walls themselves undulated.

When it quieted, I crept back inside, listening to the soft sobbing as the voice sang the song over and over, like the hum of water. The guardian slumped, his head bowed, more subdued than

I had ever seen him.

He didn't look my way; no threats, no comments about my breeding or lack thereof. There was stillness, a collapse of heart that surprised me.

When he finally spoke, a tremor of desperation spiked in his voice.

"Where did you learn that?"

I remained silent. He must know that I remembered nothing, not the name of the tune, nor even where I picked it up. But my hands remembered, my fingers knew. Some part of me recalled this from my past, a past where I had a life. A past that meant something here.

Finally, I ventured a question. "What happened? The walls moved."

He raised his eyes to me as he spoke, speaking so low that I sidled over to better hear.

"That was Roselyn."

There was such sorrow in his voice that I sat before the mirror. I crossed my legs, waiting for him to speak again.

"This Tower was once a girl, a magician, from a long line of magicians. She was beautiful and talented." He stopped speaking; I willed him to continue. He looked across at me then. "She's locked within these walls, sleeping, dreaming. Unknown to her, the havoc she wreaks."

Here he stopped, his cheeks paler than ever. I cocked my head. "So what happened?"

"Her magic twisted, changed, turned inward." He sighed deeply. "We were so close. As a child, she sat beside me as I worked, hanging on my every word, watching me conjure magic great and small."

The hair on my arms stood upright. I could feel what was coming.

"I named her Roselyn, my rose, my daughter. She was my joy,

my delight. After her mother died in childbirth, I raised her by myself here on these lands.

"When she was seventeen, a fiddle player, a simple country bumpkin from a village two days' ride from here, stole her heart. I forbade it, of course. She deserved someone better, someone of standing, of means."

I tried not to move, to say naught for fear of him stopping.

"When he offered for her, he told me that old tale of young love, of true love." The Guardian looked to me for understanding. "I refused. I sent him away, hoping that would be the end of it. But he returned over and over.

"I reasoned with Roselyn, explaining that she couldn't marry him. He came from a family of crofters, one step up from nothing, breeding children like litters of puppies. I couldn't let her go to him. Couldn't bear to think of her living like that, in a stepped-up cottage surrounded by a half-dozen grubby children. But she was entranced, unable to see how impossible it was. She only stared at me with pleading eyes.

"Finally, to end this madness, I agreed—but he must prove his worth. I said I would not let her go cheaply. I would agree to the marriage when he returned with two matched horses, one silver and one gold, one bullock burnished to copper, three hundred ducats, and ten hectares of land. Then and only then would he get my permission to wed.

"I knew it was impossible.

"He accepted my terms and left soon after, leaving her with false promises and his pledge to return. He vowed to write her every week.

"I gave him seven years. Roselyn insisted she would wait seven times seven." He looked past me, out the doors to the hills beyond.

"She was a dutiful daughter, a gentle girl, not one to scream and rage. She waited a month and then another. Six months passed, and nary a word. No letters. Her heart broke. He was fickle, just as

I predicted. He left her behind with nary a thought.

"I let it be known that Roselyn was marriageable. Many suitors came that year, offering for her hand. She was beautiful, talented, and our lands well-endowed."

I bit my lip not to point out what she had changed into.

"She could have had anyone, any number of well-positioned men.

"She refused them. Oh, she was polite, but unmovable. After nine months, she retreated into this Tower, looking out across the land, waiting for his return.

"Soon after, I noticed she was fading, her skin becoming transparent. I tried to comfort her. I urged her to travel, to meet others of her own kind, those from her station in life. She had such a gentle spirit, so much to offer. She would nod as if in agreement, her skin as translucent as the fog, and sit out on the balcony yearning for him. Each day, every week, every month she withdrew more."

He stared out beyond me, as if he could see her still.

"Toward the end of that first year, I realized she was fading into the walls of the Tower itself. As the year drew to a close, I barely stopped to eat, hoping to reach her. I pleaded again and again with her to leave this building, to sit outside in the sunlight, to travel. Anything to draw her back to the world.

"That last day, I stationed myself by her chair, gripping her hand, even as she slipped from my grasp. That next morning, she was gone, herself encased within these walls. And I, too, was caught, my magic bound within this Tower, myself locked within the mirror."

From within the walls, I heard her voice again.

I will marry at thy will, sire,
At thy will.

The guardian stopped to listen also, before he ended with, "All she does now is dream of him."

In view of the couples trapped and his daughter's misery, I could muster little sympathy for him, but still I listened. He seemed to withdraw. Then he continued.

"In the spring of the next year, a girl appeared, as you did, her memory gone. I wasn't overly concerned at first. I didn't know how to help, but I made sure she was comfortable. That she wanted for nothing. My magic, though restricted, was still sufficient for that. Then one month after, a youth came seeking her, drawn by dreams and magic. The girl called out when she recognized her love. But as he touched the walls, he, too, was trapped. Hour after hour, until the sun set, he fought. Then it was over. Both of them had been absorbed, locked into that panel over there, neither dead nor alive but captured in some half-life."

My heart stopped. I couldn't breathe.

"Since that day, right as spring breaks forth, a couple is drawn to the Tower. First a Lady and then, a month later, a man comes, pulled by forces he can't ignore.

"Roselyn doesn't know what she is doing. It is all a dream to her. I believe she seeks her fickle lover, and in her dreams, she finds others, those who love, and wishes them close."

I whispered my question, "How many times has this happened?"

"You are the seventh."

I rocked back, sure I hadn't heard that right. It couldn't be.

He was quiet and then spoke so low I could barely make it out.

"Use this time wisely. Take pleasure where you can and compose yourself for the end."

My eyebrows rose to my hairline. "The end? What end?"

Something between sadness and fear flared in his eyes. My eyes flicked to the empty panel across from me. My panel. I could deny it no longer.

"Maybe they didn't try very hard. Maybe they wanted to stay. Maybe…"

I set ready to ask a hundred questions when the sun slipped

behind a cloud. When I looked again, he had faded away.

The angry screech of an eagle pulled me out of my reverie as I stumbled out onto the balcony. A raven was tormenting the eagle, teasing it, diving and dipping in the air. He flew circles around the raptor, who clung steadfastly to a long silver fish. The raven dipped below him and rolled upside down, one hundred feet in the air, reaching one black leg upward to claw the eagle's belly. I hadn't seen that before, ever. I held my breath at such a display. At once, the raven flipped back upright, dropping away from those sharp raptor talons.

But this time, the eagle had had enough. He released his catch, pivoting downward, legs outstretched. The raven realized his danger too late. I saw a scattering of black feathers as the eagle struck the raven. The would-be black thief tumbled through the sky, spinning like a child's top before he managed to get his wings outstretched and glided lower, wobbling side to side. He landed three feet from me in an ungainly thud.

Chapter

7

It is amazing how much you can deceive yourself. Like a mouse beneath a wolf's paw, I was trapped, frozen in fear. I had suspected this for weeks yet pushed it away, as does a child who knows that beets and liver exist but still wishes to believe in a perfect world. Now, too much had happened for me to ignore. The Guardian didn't appear again, though I banged on the mirror over and over until my knuckles bled. My thoughts spilled out in a messy pile. A panel waited for me—that was to be my end. The tight bands of hope and reason that held me popped one by one. I was unraveling. My head hurt. My nose dripped tears.

Outside on my balcony, a raven lay crumpled and bruised. I tried to ignore him. Mostly, I didn't need to try, as I lay in a stunned daze for the greater part of the night. I kept my eyes turned from the battered creature outside my balcony doorway, his eyes glazed with shock, mouth open and gasping.

I had more than enough to think about without this problem.

I heard him scrabble, trying to stand, and the resulting thump as he flopped sideways again. All morning it repeated, *struggle, stritch, thump, struggle, stritch, thump.*

Shortly before noon, I exerted myself enough to put a small water-filled saucer near him. He sought to threaten me, a nasty *kaa* coming from his throat for my trouble. Still, I could bear no creature, no matter how vile, to die of thirst.

I stayed well away, numb to anything but my own predicament and terror. Within the walls, I saw the Lady again, dreaming. Her pulling felt inevitable. I should give over, stop fighting. There was no escape, no way out, no hidden doorway.

An hour passed, maybe two, until I struggled up from my despair and examined each panel, reassessing the trapped couples with my new understanding.

Stritch, thump, stritch, flutter, thump.

I bestirred myself enough to check the raven. He was standing now. Thump. Well, no longer, down again, but he had moved about two arms' length. Closer to the Tower. The walls quivered, feeling a life so near. Caught between me and the Tower wall, the bird sensed, as did most creatures, danger. I shivered and went back inside, staring again at the blank panel. My panel—the one I looked at last evening and again this morning in morbid fascination. I rubbed my eyes, still swollen from crying and lack of sleep, sure that I was seeing things. A smudge of new lines, with the faintest imprint of color. The silhouette of a body, the face blurred. Someone else was caught in Roselyn's web. Someone I loved, someone I yearned to see.

My fingers reached out of their own accord. From the adjacent panel, I heard Dulce's voice pleading over and over, "*Resist, resist.*"

I turned and walked to the balcony, pushing my way past the misty barrier that clung to me. It was increasingly difficult to leave, harder to push out those doors. I needed to feel the wind in my hair and breathe air not cloyed with the incense of the Lady's magic.

Somewhere below me lay a world untainted by the gone-awry charms for a long-disappeared suitor. But I couldn't reach it.

***

I grabbed the remains of my meal from the table inside and forced my way back outside again, bearing a crust of bread, the core of a pear, and some scraps of poached egg. As I approached the raven, he tried to scrabble away, though less than before. Maybe he was getting used to me, or maybe he was just spent.

Though he neared exhaustion, he fought. It had been a full day he lay there in pain, the same time I struggled with the knowledge of my end. I felt a bond, a fellow creature trapped, both of us doomed.

I looked down over the balcony edge, staring into the twilight gloom to the ground below. Would it be better to jump, to chance surviving, broken but alive? Even death might be better than being locked within these walls, forever trapped. Would that stop Roselyn from bringing another? From filling the last panel?

The raven moved, his tail feathers now almost touching the wall. Roselyn stirred as if in a restless dream. I could see her now if I looked slantways at the wall. Her golden hair flowed in waves to her waist. Her finger moved as if she longed for that small life so close to her exterior wall. The floor rippled, undulating as she tilted her head, her eyes still closed, her cheeks and lips soft pink as she concentrated, her fingers pulling. The raven's eyes widened; his ruff raised. In teeny increments, she pulled him closer. Both of his damaged wings braced as he resisted her magic.

I couldn't leave him to this fate. I walked over and unceremoniously picked him up. He was still pretty feisty, kaaing as they do when angry. He tried to stab me, fought, but I held him securely, big as he was, in both my hands. I pinned his wings gently against his body and kept my face well away from his sharp beak and tearing claws.

A feeling dawned over me, a creeping sense of knowing.

I had handled birds before. My hands knew how to hold him, my fingers clever and fast, as now. I had stroked the soft downy under-feathers of birds before, felt the fragile hollow bones, the satin roughness of segmented feathers. I ran my hand across the ribs of his wings, checking for breaks. Some part of me recalled this, as with the fiddle. Some part of me remembered, though from when and where I couldn't recollect. It lay beyond my mind's reach, lingering around a corner.

He quorked and struggled. I spread his left wing carefully and then his right, trying not to inflict more pain. One of his legs seemed tender. A bruised or pulled tendon maybe, but no broken ribs. A smidge of dried blood encrusted his wing, probably a cut, bloody but no fatal harm. His pinioned feather ends were tipped, two badly, but if he lived, they would regrow.

He wouldn't be flying anytime soon; he could barely stand. He would die here—like me.

Perhaps he had a chance, perhaps he could fly away. I poured some water from a porcelain pitcher onto my linen handkerchief, one embroidered with yellow daisies, and gently cleaned off the dried blood. There was a tiny gash on the underside but no debilitating damage. Nothing that, with care, couldn't heal in a few days' time.

With the raven beside me, I sat outside most of that evening and well into the night, listening to Dulce's whisper repeating, "*Resist, resist…*" I gritted my teeth against the relentless pull to go back inside that had started since the lines appeared on my panel, until I was driven inside by hunger and exhaustion. I crawled into the large bed, feeling the press of the layers and layers of bedding, and fell into a restless sleep for what little remained of the night.

Early the next morning, I awoke. Dread weighed on my mind. Spring was well on its way, and with it, my end—and someone else's. Someone who loved me. Someone whom I loved. Inadvertently, my glance landed on the last panel. The shadow of an additional body deepened, growing more defined, even in the soft morning light.

I ate the breakfast that appeared, saving some for the raven, before I shoved my way onto the balcony and checked on him. Made sure he had water, made sure he was nowhere near the wall. He was better, no longer gasping in shock, now calm enough to watch me with a wary eye. He struggled some, not much, exhausted and more accustomed to my presence. He remained too weak to do much damage to me but appeared aware of his dilemma. Ravens are wickedly clever, nasty, but very savvy and canny. He knew that food came from my hands and that I had aided him. I gentled him again, checking that he was outside of Roselyn's grasp before I went back inside to brood.

I lay back on the bed watching within the wall as the Lady's hands wove, braiding strands of air that sought and captured any life nearby. I curled into a ball, pulling the coverlet over my head, trying to block out her image. My hair plait unraveled.

I kicked off the bedding and pressed my hands against my forehead. The curtains swayed in the light breeze from the windows. The raven outside, resisting, trying to survive. Part of my mind repeated over and over, *No escape, no escape.* My brain wouldn't stop. It attached itself to images, flipping from thing to thing, not able to hold on to any. Couples, raven, braid, plaits, weaving. My hands tightened on the bed curtain, and I ripped it. I ran my thumb across the grain of a single finger's width strip, feeling its strength. I ripped another and then another. Five strands of silk, strong silk. I started a braid, a simple child's garland of over and under. I tugged at it after I had gone about a forearm's length. It was strong, but would it hold my weight?

Chapter

8

The Guardian watched while I ripped bed curtains, drapes, and sheets into strips. He'd seemed subdued since he told me his story; no wraiths, no clacking of bells.

"You can't leave."

"I can." I didn't bother looking up but continued shredding the bedding into long two- finger-wide strips. Surrounding me were lengths of silk, cotton, and linen. Some woven into rope and some lying in heaps.

His voice wavered. "This won't work, you know. It's too far. You'll never be able to make it long enough."

"Maybe nae, but 'twill be better than jumping from here," I retorted.

"It will break as soon as you put your weight on it."

"Then I will definitely be closer to the ground, won't I."

He squinted at me as a cloud sauntered by, veiling the sun. "She won't let you leave. The moment you try to escape the Tower, she'll know."

I rounded on him. "What dae ye care? You're in cahoots with her."

He blinked as if surprised.

I went back to my rope braiding. "Ye could help me."

He dismissed my words, launching into his own concerns. "Before you try something rash, let's look at this another way. What about that tune you played? Where did you learn it? Think. Try to remember."

I glared at him. "I have tried. Remember what ye said. My memory was removed as a *kindness*. I cannae recall a thing," I hissed. I turned away slowly, dismissing him, my back tingling with the force of his gaze, and continued weaving my rope.

"Wait." I spun back around. "You'd heard it before. Ye *knew* that tune. The one that I played the other day. Where did *ye* first hear it? Do ye know why *she* reacted?"

The lines in his face deepened. He didn't speak, so still and silent I wondered if he had changed to granite.

Finally, he whispered, "*He* played it. Will. He wrote it for her, and they played it as a duet. 'A love song for two musicians,' she told me."

I shivered, wondering how I could have heard Roselyn's tune. A melody my fingers knew, even with my memory gone.

"She hummed it hour after hour when he first left until it grated on my nerves."

Maybe this was an answer. "So, what dae ye think would happen if I played it again?" I glanced over my shoulder at the fiddle lying peacefully tossed on a tasseled, sapphire-blue pillow.

I had thought he was so white he could get no paler, but he did. Snow owl white.

"You saw. She searched for him. This whole building was pulling apart, stone by stone. We all could die."

We stayed in uncompanionable silence. I went back to my

braiding, testing the strength of the strips in my hands.

"You're only fooling yourself by doing this."

I turned away from him again to re-examine one pile. I didn't think it would hold my weight. What if I mixed the silk with the cotton? Would that strengthen it enough? I glanced at the mirror. He was waiting for a response.

"So ye said. But I dinnae intend to be one more in her collection of wall art. Ye can stay and dust the windowsills if ye want."

"What about the other ladies and their gentlemen?" He jabbed a hand toward the walls. "Are you willing to jeopardize their existence by your impetuousness? They're trapped here, waiting. Who knows what would happen if someone left? The Tower itself might be destroyed."

"How would that be a bad thing?" I stood up and paced between the mirror and the picture of the couple in the pond. My skin crawled with my new understanding. "Are ye truly alive? You're trapped here, living in some weird half-life. Whatever magic this is, 'tis broken, locked in some dark nightmare of Roselyn's mind. Nae one without magic can fix it." I thought about Dulce; her voice had comforted me, and I wondered if she would rather die or continue as a ghostly parlor-maid. Or was she already dead? I shivered.

"Not true. What do you think I do when I'm not working to make your life more bearable here? Where do you think the food and clothes come from? The clean silk bedding, the tea steeped just the right amount, the dresses that fit you perfectly. It's my work. I still have power, and I can reach her. Every day my time is spent working this riddle, at breaking the locks, undoing the tangle of her magic."

I raised my voice. "I dinnae want your silly dresses and perfect tea! I never asked for it. The only thing I truly need is to get out of here." I jerked my hands at the overskirt of the petal pink gown I was wearing. Unbidden tears spilled from my eyes. "I dinnae want this. I dinnae need this. I'm going to die, entombed alive in these walls, and ye congratulate yourself that I'll be properly encased in a frilly dress?" I was crying now, loud hiccupping sobs, and unable to stop.

"You've had seven years to fix what ye caused. How long dae ye need? How many lives are to be embedded in this living shrine to your daughter before you figure out ye cannae fix it?" I felt hot with rage and wild with fear. My hands bunched into a fist. My arms tight against my sides. He blinked at me, surprised by the intensity and direction of my anger. I kicked at the piles of coiled strips that lay beside me like limp snakes.

He frowned. "This isn't my fault. It's Will's. It was Will who caused her to want to leave me. Will who made her unhappy. I stayed with her." He shook his head as if pushing away my attack, trying to justify what he had done.

"He left and never returned. I gave him a chance to win her. I protected her. She should have forgotten him. I kept his letters from her. I even tried to blank her memory." He looked up then, checking to see if I'd noticed what he had confessed.

My voice dropped to a whisper. "That's why, isn't it? She knew what ye were trying, and she fought ye."

He shook his head in denial.

"Oh, nae out loud. Nae so ye could hear, but in the only way she could. That's why she retreated into the Tower. Why she calls and traps couples in the wall. So, she will nae forget!"

Tears continued escaping, running down to my chin, leaving trails of wetness. Cold barren misery settled in my chest; an emptiness where his words echoed repeatedly. For the first time, I felt sorry for Roselyn. It joined and merged into a great bucket of sorrow: for her, for those locked in the wall, and for me.

I glared at The Guardian. "'Tis all your fault. Your word isn't worth the spit from a stoat. You're a villain. Ye caused this, and now she locked herself up here. Well, ye can keep her, but I'm leaving, with or without your help."

I didn't need to stay to see his astonished face. I marched outside, or at least pushed, as the mist there had thickened into a gel. I had to beat and shove my way through, as it stuck to my skin like a spider's web of vines. I pushed harder, hitting my hands against it, kicking with my feet. Finally, I popped into the cold night air, shocking the raven into a belated quork. Right before I fainted.

Chapter

9

Some time after the sun lifted her bloodshot eye above the horizon, I awoke shivering with cold to my hair being pulled. I opened my eyelids to see small, black, wise pupils. The raven stared back at me and rasped out a quork, demanding his breakfast. I extended my hand toward him, and he hopped clumsily away before cautiously reapproaching, turning his head from side to side, examining my fingernails. Limping a step or two around as if he, too, was critical of my looks. I raised myself upon one elbow, looking out across the greening landscape. The raven shook out his ruff and hopped beside me. We spent a few moments evaluating one another: he seeing me as a potential bringer of food; me seeing him as a fellow prisoner. It was a bonding of sorts. I picked myself up and trundled inside, a concession to the cold that nipped my nose and fingers.

I watched the drawing within my panel; more lines appeared and shading filled in the shadows. The lines darkened: a lass, very young and skinny-legged; a man, clean shaven and then—I blinked—a third image, a woman, waves of hair spilling down. I went back to each of the other panels and counted. Two, two, two, two, two, two. Never were there more. I circled back. My panel was changing. The lines etching into the stone. I resisted the desire to touch it, the deadly yearning to lean into the drawing.

Definitely, there were three; three silhouettes deep in my panel. Roselyn sat up now, smiling. A look of happy expectancy and hope crossed her face. I crouched before it.

The drawing cleared enough now for me to make out details, now that color overlaid the lines. A man. His hair was dark, like mine, with eyes of blue and a determined chin, unhidden by face hair. The other figure was Roselyn—it had to be. With that long golden hair, there was no mistaking her. In the panel, she reached out and smiled at the man. A dark-haired child sat nearby, playing with a toy, a wooden bird perhaps, a younger, smaller version of me. I couldn't be older than seven or eight. I leaned closer. It wasn't a toy, 'twas a merlin, and I knew his name: Sunshine.

That's when I noticed yet another change. Over in the farthest corner, another figure, a fourth, began to form, just a smudge of line, a hand reaching out toward… what? I fell back on my heels.

Now I was confused.

I put those thoughts aside and focused on the real problem. If I didn't leave soon, I would never leave. If the darkening lines on the image were any indication, it was time, past time, for me to escape. I sat forward, elbows on my knees. Before I could reconsider, I got up, grabbed the braided, spliced rope, tied it to the bedpost now notched with twenty-seven cuts and battered my way back to the balcony.

Behind me, I could hear the Guardian call out. "Child, don't do this. Give me a little more time, a week, less even."

In the stillness that followed, I thought I heard Dulce speak.

I ignored them both. I wrapped the rope about my body, settling it snugly across my back, pulling the braids of cloth across my chest so I could ease myself down. The raven hopped toward me. He and I stared at one another. Blowing air through my pursed lips, I conceded. I threw together a sling from the ripped-off bottom of my lace petticoat and stuffed him in it.

I tested the rope and pulled again. It seemed sturdy. I put tension on it, climbed onto the metal balcony railing, and levered myself over the edge.

Nightmarish images assailed me. Monsters crawled below, leaping and reaching for me. Great bone-tearing beasts slavering for my body. Mouths with teeth the size of drumsticks and eyes that glowed awaited me. Not safety, not freedom. I froze in place and checked the raven. He showed no sense of fear as he peered around cheerfully, like a babe swaddled at its mother's breast. In the stillness of the moment, I thought I heard Dulce's voice again, and this time I heard what she said: '*Resist.*'

Nothing was there to harm me. Roselyn's illusions only. I breathed deep, trying to calm myself, releasing the rope slowly from my hands, carefully removing my feet from the railing until I dangled midair. I knew better than to let my body touch the wall, that sticky trap that pulled and absorbed anything it touched.

As I slid downward, Roselyn's image within the stone seemed to follow me, her face taut with anguish. Her voice started up again:

Rose, Rose, Rose, Rose.

The Tower shook itself like a wet dog, and I wobbled, trying to avoid contact with Roselyn's snare.

Will I ever see thee wed?

From inside the wall, the golden-haired woman closed her hand, and my chest clenched. Sharp slicing pain racked me. My back arched, and I fought a scream. I struggled against her, biting my lip to resist the pain.

The Lady tugged harder, her eyes still closed, a frown marring her finely drawn brow. I tried to inhale. I couldn't breathe.

I will marry at thy will, sire

At thy will.

Strands of webbing pressed against my lungs, wrapping itself around my chest, tight and cold.

From far inside the Tower, the Guardian called out. "No, Roselyn, no. Don't."

The pressure eased, and air rushed into my lungs. I could feel blood run down my chin from biting my lips, but I could breathe again and I restarted my rappel. Tears streamed down my cheeks as renewed pain assailed me. *Don't let go, don't let go,* I thought, forcing myself to let out the rope slowly. Again.

Above, I could hear the Guardian pleading with Roselyn as she continued to sing. "Listen to me, Roselyn, no one has actually died yet. This isn't who you are."

I kept my focus on my rope, let it out, let it slip across my body, as I lowered myself toward the ground, letting the rope travel through my hands. Not too fast. The Tower vibrated as Roselyn sobbed. Down ten feet. Again, she attacked, and I couldn't breathe. I kept going a smidgeon faster. Ten more feet. My chest hurt, and I was dizzy with the need for air. A jolt shook the Tower, and the Guardian called out, "I can hold her for but a handful of time more. Go!"

The pressure on my chest eased, and I sucked in air. My face taut with pain, I shimmied down another dozen feet. My shoulders ached, the muscles in my arms shuddered with exhaustion. Ten feet and twenty more. How much farther could the ground be? Above, I heard an anguished cry, and my chest felt crushed. Down five feet. I tried to inhale. The pain was too great. Two feet more. My hands slipped, and I grabbed tighter as I slid, ignoring the burning of my palms. No air. How much farther? I heard a pop. One strand of my spliced rope frayed and snapped. Da would be so disgusted with my workmanship.

Da! I remembered!

Above me, the Guardian yelled out another command. Before

I let go, to have it be over, my lungs expanded with air.

I clenched my hands and screamed as the rope skinned them. I hung for a minute, dangling, taking in gasps of air. Cautiously, I looked down. Only ten feet left. Nothing. Roselyn let fly a handful of stones from the Tower as I slid the rest of the way and landed on my back. The raven wriggled in my sling but stayed put. Quickly, I rolled out from Roselyn's range, taking in deep gulping breaths and listening to her sobs.

Chapter

10

Roselyn's cries started within minutes of my escape. I needed to get away before I was caught again.

My stomach tightened as Roselyn pleaded, wooing me back with unspecified promises that drew me like a moth to a flame. But I knew what waited there. I considered the fate of the Guardian, Dulce, and the others, trapped. I pushed those thoughts away. I couldn't think about them. They needed a hero, someone with magic. Not me. With a farewell fist to the Tower, I clenched my teeth and turned away.

But a skip from where I landed was the grand house, far enough from the Tower that I felt I could stop and catch my breath. Away from Roselyn's immediate reach, but too close for me to linger.

I had observed this house while in the Tower, watched birds go in and out, a fox leave with a fat dove in his mouth. Some pall of foreboding kept my kind away from this property. No one had lived there for some time; windows missed panes and rafters peeled away. A garden filled with runaway roses climbed arbors crooked with age.

It must have been wondrous once, with towering walls of cypress, cocooning beds of flowers. But now weeds competed with the emerging leaves of hundreds of daffodils and crocus. Mignonette lined the pathways overgrown with the spiky blue bracts of Miss Wilmott's Ghost. Out back, the sad remains of a vegetable garden straggled along. Thistles, brambles, and Queen Anne's Lace overran what must have been an imposing garden. Some ferny plants formed a hedge. I inched closer, investigating the familiar green shoots—asparagus, none other.

As I plopped the raven down, he objected with a loud gronk, though he stayed put. I harvested an armful of the asparagus and then paused long enough to eat a handful of alpine strawberries before pitching a couple toward the raven, who deigned to accept them. It was a feast for kings, perhaps not up to my standards for the past month, but enough to carry me 'til mid-day.

My single recollection of Da danced in my brain. I tilted my head, hoping for more memories to come trotting in, but no, nothing. Finally, I gave up and walked forward.

At the entrance to the mansion, I hesitated. My heart still slammed against my chest from fear. I checked behind me. Was this also a trap? Nothing here pulled at me. Nothing reeked of Roselyn's magic. After walking a wide circle around the door, I dismissed that thought upon seeing animal tracks both going in and leaving. Spring or not, it could be a long walk and many nights outside in bad weather. I needed supplies to survive.

Inside were rooms with stone floors covered with thick rugs. Paintings with gilt frames lined the walls. Silver candelabras, tarnished black, and crystal sconces crusted with dust. Once, it must have been quite the fancy place, but now beds were covered with the tatters of moth-eaten coverlets, slathered with a layer of rat and bird dung—the musty smell stung my nose—rat droppings everywhere.

The raven looked intrigued as we both heard the scurrying of small feet. He hopped from my shoulder and limped around, dragging his bruised left leg, peering into corners, checking the premises like a proud new bride inspecting her marriage home. He tossed small things aside as if looking for the perfect gift. I heard a squeak and turned to see a young rat, furless and naked, tossed into the air and disappearing down his gullet. A small tail stuck out as he swallowed. Almost immediately, another rodent shared that fate. A gathering of cockroaches joined them. In the kitchen, I scraped off the top layer of grunge from around the hearth and smeared the uncovered fat across my rope-burned palms.

I stiffened my shoulders and stepped through the long grand hall. Once, it must have glittered like snow on a pine. I was disgusted at the filth and was eager to be away, but first I needed to collect what I could for the journey. Rifling through the kitchen shelves, I found the essentials: some flint, a cup, a hunting knife, its edge still sharp. In a cedar-lined chest, I found some boy's trousers, shirt, and a suede jerkin dyed an odd color of green. A pair of boots, the leather cracked and dry, sat at the bottom of an armoire. They were a size too big, but I stuffed them with felting. The mound grew as I sorted through armoires and chests.

I pursed my lips and blew out a whistle as I studied the pile. The raven repeated the whistle. I whistled again. Three notes this time. Again, he imitated me. I knew ravens were mimics. I remembered tracking a covey of partridge only to round a corner and hear the ruckus kaaing of ravens, voices as shrill as if they were laughing at me. But here I conversed with a raven that joined me as I whistled. And I thought he also talked back.

I inspected my stack of belongings. It was too much for me to carry. I started another pile, discarding everything that wasn't essential.

Twice, I turned to the Tower, responding to Roselyn's calls, and twice, the raven flew at me, awakening me as if from an enchantment. I needed to be gone, as far as I could get from this place. Away from the Tower, the Guardian, even Dulce and the other wraiths. Away from my fears and my guilt for the ones who didn't escape, who were there forever.

The Tower gleamed like burnished metal in the sunlight, the walls thicker than a battering ram could dent, its slick sides making it impossible to climb, walls that grabbed anything that touched them.

The lair of a golden-haired magician who dreamed of love lost. The image of the trapped wraiths scurried through my mind. My body shook as I recalled how close I had been to joining them.

Again, I tried to shrug it off; there was nothing I could do. It was a hero's task or a magician's, and I was but a lass.

I went back to my packing, resisting Roselyn's urgings by continuing with my own litany, a list of what I needed to get home. A cap of linen, sturdy enough to withstand the forest wilds, and the most wonderful wool cloak in a soft fawn brown, moth-eaten and stinking of mildew but large enough to wrap myself twice around on a cold night. It was heavy, but without it, I didn't stand a chance of surviving a turn in the weather. Before I left, I filled my ears with bee's wax from a burnt-down candle.

I hefted my pack, lifted the raven to my shoulder, and trotted down the weed-encroached road. Behind me, I dimly could hear Roselyn's keening, pulsing begin as if her world had ended.

But mine had begun again.

Chapter

11

I awakened early, my finger smarting from the sharp nip of an impatient raven. I had walked for most of the previous day, pushing hard to get far from the Tower and glorying in my freedom. Still, I'd glanced over my shoulder more than once. I wasn't sure why. Did I fear Roselyn's siren call, or was it my guilt for leaving Dulce?

I'd camped at a small rivulet not far off the road, ate my dinner, and promptly fell asleep. A night free of dread and wraiths. Only the crickets to sing me to sleep.

Dusty and sore, I awoke pleased with myself. I had truly escaped. I trudged down the road, my raven's talons clamped on my shoulder's padding. He was too big to fit there comfortably, but with his wing outstretched for balance and his tail crooked down my back, he watched the upcoming road like a scout. He tugged at a strand of my hair and tweaked my earlobe if I paused for any length of time, murmuring guttural raven instructions into my ear. Bound by circumstance, we were becoming good friends. I was rethinking my opinions of ravens. The two of us had escaped certain death. Maybe ravens weren't so horrible. I whistled a tune, and the raven joined, adding a husky trill to punctuate each phrase. He was clever.

An image flittered into my head: a man, dark-haired, shooting arrows at a flock of ravens. And me, a skinny lass, cheering him on, with a hooded and jessed merlin on my arm. So perhaps I hadn't been overly fond of ravens then—but I was growing partial to this one.

With that recollection, my mind whipped back to Sunshine, my merlin, the first hawk I trained as my own. He was wonderful. With his unerring flight and keen eyesight, he never flew from my arm without returning with his quarry.

And then it came to me, my name, Nell Pritchard of Sweethaven. I raised up my hand and danced like some Romani traveler for a few steps, unsettling the raven on his precarious perch. I knew my name!

I tripped over memories that piled up one after the other. Da, Mam, little Tim, Ben, who struggled to overcome his fear of climbing, Hal, Cam, insufferably cocky, and Ned, apprenticed last year as a blacksmith journeyman.

And Will, my favorite brother, gone seven years. He had been the first to note I had a skill and the one who guided me in climbing and training my hawk.

I sobered. Was he alive or dead? He left even before Tim was born.

It hit me then, and I stumbled in surprise. Will! Will and Roselyn. It was she he had courted. It wasn't my sweetheart who she hunted. Roselyn had hit pay dirt with me. She was pulling my brother, someone I loved. But her lover, not mine. She wanted him, and I was her bait.

To be sure, I remembered those days. Trailing along behind my brother with my merlin on my shoulder, so proud was I of my first hawk. Will convinced Da to give me a chance. Will climbed to the aerie and brought down the bundle of downy feathers that was my first bird.

And I *had* proved myself. Sunshine surpassed all the rich merchants' birds that year. Bringing in prey after prey. Always returning to my arm.

Da patted me on the back, conceding I was a natural falconer. My eight-year-old self had burst with pride when he sold. My money provided an actual silver coin for us. Never again was I relegated to the kitchen.

I picked up my pace. Mam was over six months with child before I was taken. Shivers ran down my back. Mam's last birthing had ended badly, and no one could help. Please, let it live, not like Mam's last birth. And please, please, let it be a lass this time.

As I broke into a trot, I calculated over a month lost to this place, to magic, and nothing to show for it. I had sworn to Da I would get more hawks to sell for the spring fair. He and I hoped to win the fair prize and have money for a doctor for Mam's birthing this time. Most hawks would have fledged and flown by now. My heart sank.

The road bumped along untended down a great hill, and more memories rolled in like water spilling over a miller's dam. I remembered visiting that mansion. Will brought me there many times. The line of juniper and cedars formed a break from the winds, protecting the gardens and the mansion. I came there with him while he was courting a lass, a rich lass.

A flash of copper feathers of a ring-necked pheasant amidst the gorse distracted me. My mouth watered, thinking of the sweet dark meat. I needed food.

***

I lay back, finishing off a quite satisfactory meal of fiddlehead ferns roasted under a bed of coals. A tad charred, perhaps, but fine after I flicked off the worst of the burned bits. The raven inspected my leavings with all the indignation of a noble.

My head turned, listening for any further sound from Roselyn, but only the trees sighed and the birds called.

Now that I was out, free of the Tower, I pondered that last panel with its darkening lines. I was as sure as a stone is hard that it was Will she wanted. Will, she was calling. I was only a lure, laid out as carefully as any trapper might do to entrap my brother.

But there had been the hint of one other. Was that true or merely my mind playing tricks? I put it aside. My ears packed with moss, I set off again. Whatever had been in that panel no longer mattered; I'd broken free. I no longer was bait. No one need come for me. Will was gone seven years, far, far from here. And I was homeward bound.

Still, I checked my back a dozen times, made sure I headed away from the Tower, all the time wondering if Roslyn's magic could grab me again, how it had in the first place. My stomach tightened with the thought, and I banished it. It wouldn't happen again, not ever!

On my second day out, the road tracked alongside a stream cascading into a clear pond. It opened up to a small grassy clearing that called for rest. My hair felt lank and greasy. My skin grimed from walking long hours. It was too much to resist. I stripped down to my silk small clothes and threw myself in, hollering as I hit the cold water. The raven limped into the shallows, lifting up small stones in his search for food. He voiced his displeasure over the choices with the varied grumblings of ravens.

It was early to make camp, but my legs were sore and my stomach rumbled. I felt more tired than I should from a mere fifteen miles or so of walking. A blister had burst on my big toe. I had become soft during my stay in the Tower.

But this pond was familiar, only twelve miles out from home. A trip I had made with Will many times before he left, before the first lassie's disappearance and all had changed.

Most people feared magicians, that half handful of people with unknown power, but not Will. He trusted everyone, believed that everyone was as honest and open as he was. Like Da. There was a natural charm about him, a way of being that made the most cankerous neighbor smile when he walked by.

But that was before Will left and the magician's fog descended upon those who walked this road, rendering them addled and fearful for a season after. Before lads and lasses disappeared and never returned.

I missed Will, missed his kindness and the half-smile that transformed his face, missed the comfort of his hand on my shoulder when I felt unsure.

A good night's rest, an early start tomorrow, and I would be home before dinner. Beneath a cluster of elm trees, I crouched, roasting seven silver trout over my fire embers. The stream was so plentiful with fish, they had all but launched themselves into my hands. The raven hobbled nearby, ripping a fish into bits.

My hair lay limp and damp against my neck. I stretched out, wiggling my toes from the sheer pleasure of being free. The raven screeched, and I leapt to my feet at the sound of hoofbeats.

As a horse emerged from the dark green shadow of trees, I relaxed. Its rider wasn't a threat; he was dropping dead in the saddle. Unkempt beard, head down, his shoulders slanted as if he'd been too many hours without a rest. He rode a horse, some unknown hue darkened with layers of mud and lather dried across withers and legs; and led a dappled grey. They pulled at the reins as he passed by the stream. Froth encrusted on their mouths.

I couldn't bear anyone treating their stock like that. "Hey, mister, your horses are beat. Nae use killing them and ye both."

He didn't seem to hear me. I thought perhaps he dozed on his horse. "If ye keep pushing, neither ye nor your horses will get where ye are going." I returned to stuffing another piece of trout in my mouth. "Ye might as well join me."

He heard me then, jerked upright. Two knives appeared in his hands as his head lifted and a snarl crossed his face. I jumped. Perhaps he wasn't as harmless as he seemed. I scrambled back, wondering if I had jabbed a hornet's nest.

I felt his glare pierce me just before his knives tumbled from his hands onto the soft earth. His eyes rolled up inside his head, and he slowly slid off the horse. Though he didn't move, I hesitated to touch him. The knives I kicked away in case he came to. I stepped closer. Would he leap up and grab me? Finally, when he didn't move, I couldn't bear it. Someone had to help this traveler, and no one else was around.

He was limp as a newly born lamb, but way heavier. I settled for straightening his legs before covering him with my cloak. Once I was sure he was breathing and comfortable, I raced to grab the horses.

By the time I got back to him, I had my hands full. The horses were uncatchable, but I had chased them out of the stream they rushed for before they could overwater themselves. Too good of horseflesh to let ruin.

The man lay where he had fallen, breathing heavily, though he hadn't moved since he first crumpled to the ground. His overcoat was dark and stained with sweat. I knelt to ease it off him and cursed at the sticky wetness. My hands pulled away, red and damp.

Blood trailed down his right side. I removed his long-paneled coat, looking for damage. I found it. A fresh stab wound not more than a day old. "Bollocks and double bollocks."

I whistled through my teeth. This wasn't what I was good at, but I couldn't leave him here alone. With any movement, he might bleed to death before I returned with help.

My escape hadn't gotten me far. Until this man either healed or died, I was stuck.

Part II
Home

Chapter

12

Blood stained the torn scrap as I wiped the wound once again. I hated caring for sick folks. I didn't like sitting that long, didn't like cooing over bedsides and definitely didn't like not having supplies to make him well. If only Mam was here. He needed stitching, proper bedding, and hot soup. The gash, the width of a stiletto knife blade, kept opening. Someone had roughed him up proper. From his reaction when I startled him, I would bet my hawks that someone else had some healing to do as well.

"Why cannae things go easy?" I heard myself saying to the raven. I believe he understood. The raven cocked his head and bobbed up and down in what seemed like agreement—at least in my sleep deprived state, it did.

The man lay quietly on the ground, cushioned on his saddle blanket, wrapped in my cape, his face layered with grime and beard, locked in some feverish dream.

Keeping a cautious eye on him, I rechecked his horses. They

stayed close. The one he had ridden often nuzzled him as if the man was its colt. Whenever I approached, they grew suspicious, rolling their eyes and sidling away. Now the horses grazed on the short spring grass that flourished by the stream's edge. Every so often, they would lift their heads and look over at the hurt man as if awaiting a signal.

The gray almost tripped on his lead dragging on the ground. I picked myself up and forced myself to deal with them again. After three hours of trotting around in ever more frustrating circles and facing flattened ears and bared teeth, I gave up. I settled for watching them while mulling over the past two days. The man remained conked out.

As I rewashed his wound, I turned to the raven, who appeared interested in what I had to say. "Asleep or awake, naught could be better. Nae gift, nae silver teapot, nor grand clothes can match my delight at escaping that Tower." The raven looked skeptical. "Yes, I know I've been carping. I'm tired and worried, and I want to get home. I cannae save Roselyn. She's, um, nae herself. But him—" I pointed to the man lying on the cape, my cape. "I dinnae know his story or what happened. I cannae leave a sick man to die out here."

The raven didn't seem to agree. Once I got the laddie home, somebody would take him away, find his kin. But here I was and none other was around to help. No one could walk away from something like this.

The raven preened his feathers, then bobbed up and down.

"But I can tell ye about Roselyn and Will. Don't know if ye overheard the Guardian, but that's how this started." The raven jumped as a spark popped in the fire.

"Will's my brother—my favorite brother," I explained. The raven turned his head as if understanding.

"Are ye a female? Did ye grow up with all brothers also?" The raven croaked, and I decided that he was a she. Us lassies. Yeah, that felt right, with a color like the dust from a fireplace. Soot! "Ah,

Soot, then ye understand what it's like to be in a family of all boys. You know, they lord it over ye, tease ye whenever ye try to keep up, or pat ye on the head like a puppy.

"Even your da treats you like a toy 'cause you're a lass and your mam tries to keep you in petticoats." The raven gave a croak. There seemed agreement between us.

"Will changed all that. He curried my talent with raptors. Once he let me handle one of his birds and it flew to my arm, I was hooked. He taught me to climb, how to 'man' a hawk, how to use a lure. Otherwise, I would have been scrubbing floors, cooking, and spinning like all the other lassies in my village.

"My life would have been very different if he hadn't taken a liking to me." I tossed out a piece of fish, and he snapped it up. "Will took me everywhere. That's how Roselyn knew about me. I was their chaperone." The raven let out a raucous laugh.

"Laugh all you want, but a rowdy eight-year-old can put off the most amorous of couples."

The man groaned and struggled to sit up. I stirred the fire embers, checking on this morning's catch sizzling in the ashes. I frowned. Burned again. I shrugged. It was time to force some food into him.

I didn't look forward to it. It was much like having a new baby, only bigger and meaner. Thrice during the night, he had roused. He had crawled to his knees, gibbering. I tried to settle him back down. It wasn't an easy process. He raved about robbers and took a sucker punch at me. I had the bruise to prove it.

His thrashing kept me up half the night. I wasn't used to being awakened every hour; nor was the raven. She snapped at him like I wanted to. We were both exhausted.

The sun popped up earlier than it seemed reasonable. The wound re-opened and bled again. I pressed moss against it, hoping it would seal. Who could have done this? Stabbed a man and left him for dead?

The raven and I continued our conversation. She was the only one who could understand what I was going through. "Somehow, we have to get this man back to town, back to his own people."

I checked him again. His hair was dark under the sweat and dirt. Hard to make out his face with that beard, but his mouth, what I could see of it, seemed kind. No one came this way willingly since people had started disappearing. Was he also trapped by Roselyn? But he couldn't be: all the panels were complete. Only mine was empty, with a place for my brother.

I knelt at the man's side, peering into his face, suspicious. He looked nothing like my brother. Will was clean-shaven and younger, filled with buoyancy and joy that age wouldn't diminish. Even gone seven years, I would have recognized him. Wouldn't I?

Maybe, like with Soot, Roselyn threw a wide net that trapped anyone within miles of the Tower. That would explain it. I stared at his face again, wondering if there was a hint of my brother's face in that tangle of hair and beard.

His hands moved restlessly, and my eyes fixed on his fingers. Thick calluses covered the fingers on his left hand. I looked at mine, disbelieving. This man was a musician, a fiddler probably.

I whistled an old tune, one of the first that Will had taught me to play. The raven joined in, adding some new notes toward the end of each phrase.

The man stirred, a frown puckering his brow. His eyes opened; blue eyes. The hairs on my arms stood on alert.

He turned his head, his eyes clearing for a moment. "I know you, don't I?"

As if that was all the energy he had, he collapsed back into sleep.

I watched him then, daring to hope. It had to be Will. Who else would be upon this road? Searching his face against my seven-year-old memory of my brother, I sat there quieter than ever in my life watching the fire crackle, the logs fall apart into ash. As the moon stalked across the starlit sky, I fell into a restless sleep.

***

When next I opened my eyes, he had awakened. Now he leaned on one elbow, a sheen of sweat covering his forehead, staring at me. It was early, the sun not quite breaking the early morning dark.

"Nell." He hesitated. "It is you, isn't it?"

I nodded, unable to speak, aware of my breath caught deep in my chest as shivers charged up and down my spine.

"Where's Mam?"

I wiggled into a sitting position and sat with my mouth open.

He tried focusing his eyes on me, taking in my face and hair. "You grew up while I was gone." A hint of a grin crossed his mouth. "I always knew you would be a beauty. Roselyn swore she could see your future." And then he sunk back into the pain and delirium that had kept him captive in the past days.

My brother, Will. I stared at the drawn stranger lying before me, sick and feverish, unsure of this turn of events. In the distance, Roselyn picked up her calling, sent her voice swirling with the wind. She wanted him still. A fierceness filled me; he was mine now. Mine and my family's—and no one was taking him.

Now that I knew, I saw hints of my brother. The eyes, when opened, were that particular shade of cornflower blue all our family sported. I placed a hand on his forehead and felt the beginnings of a fever.

Oh, bollocks.

When I next checked Will, I thought about what he had said. What future had Roselyn seen: for me in the Tower, me tending my brother's wounds or—me delivering Will to her? Quickly, I hunted for more moss and stuffed it in his ears.

Chapter

13

After hearing the nearby howling of creatures in the night, I determined to get us on our way. Will awoke and ate without a fight. Though he passed out soon after, I took that as good. The gash still bled. The moss peeled off dark with blood. It wouldn't close. I replaced the moss, pressing hard against his wound. *It had to close.* I needed help, and soon.

Soot and I looked over at the horses, planning how we would get onto them. The only horse we had ever owned was a sour dispositioned plow horse. He ended his years on our dinner plate after keeling over from colic.

After five tries, I got Will on the gray horse. Will, more or less awake, bade the creature to stand stock-still while I pushed, prodded, and heaved him over his back, whereupon Will drifted in and out of clarity. The other, a yellowish horse, remained suspicious of me, snapping his teeth too close to my arm before dancing beyond my reach. He never strayed far from Will's side but kept a careful distance from me. Even with Will's coaxing, it took me the better part of the morning to scramble on.

Initially, I thought to ride with Will behind, but within a mile, Will, half-asleep, turned the gray back toward the Tower. We lost much time as I rounded them up again. Finally, I tied his reins to my saddle and continued on.

Not two hours later, we had to stop before Will fell off and did himself more damage. Though we were but half a day's ride from home, he couldn't continue without rest. And I daren't leave him alone for a night.

I led the horses off the trail and laid out a horse blanket for Will. Within minutes of dismounting, he fell into a deep sleep.

That's when I heard the screeching.

Off to our side was a rocky cliff, and above were raptors, the very best peregrines. Da would just die to have some to sell this year.

There were those who would pay good money for trained peregrines. And coin meant a healer for Will and a midwife like the rich folk had for Mam.

I debated. Will needed to sleep. Nothing I could do whilst he slept. As tired as I felt, this was too good an opportunity to miss. I could make up for my lost time and still get birds ready for the fair.

I turned my head toward the sound till I picked up the bird's flight and continued tracking it until I saw his aerie. I was sure of capturing nestlings before Will roused again. It was a quick sprint up the cliff, nothing!

I checked Will again, making him as comfortable as I could with a saddle for a pillow and a blanket to keep away the chill. His ears were as packed with moss as I could reasonably do. After a moment's thought, I tied a rope from his ankle to a sturdy tree in the off-chance he roused before I finished. The horses I unsaddled but left on their bridles. There was fresh grass easily reached so they could forage.

Will didn't open his eyes. He slept, worn from the little distance we had covered. I'd be up and back before he woke.

I had made it most of the way up when my foot slipped on the rock face. "Bollocks!" This should have been an easy harvest.

I peeked down. Will lay seventy-five feet below me, out cold, exhausted from the few hours of travel we had put in today.

Now that I dangled by one hand, my plan didn't seem as clever as it had when I stood with both my feet firmly on the ground. I gritted my teeth and swung my other arm, reaching, digging my fingertips into a nick of the rock. One foot fought for purchase, raveling small stones down. I pulled my chin level with the next ledge, braced my feet, and breathed.

Four chicks turned to stare. They were older than I expected, fledged, and eager to defend their aerie. One of them launched himself at me, and I barely dodged his attack.

Balancing like a traveling performer, I grabbed him and stuffed him in my jerkin, hoping the dark would quiet him while I finished. The others took to screeching for their parents. I wanted mine too. I hoped I could get down from here before theirs returned. I snuck in a quick glance across the sky, then pursed my lips in a scowl. Bollocks. Off in the distance, falcons winged toward me. What was the chance that they weren't the parents? With the luck I'd been having, none.

A final stretch, and I grabbed one more chick, adding him to his disgruntled sibling before rapidly descending.

I was halfway down when I heard voices. Rich folks with their clipped vowels.

"Hey, boy."

I kept my focus on placing my feet and hands, ignoring the snotty-nosed lad who called. My arms were scraped and bruised from prickles and gorse. I knew now where I had gotten my bruises. They were come by honorably, climbing cliffs and training raptors.

Another voice chimed in. "Are you in need of help?"

"Just like you, Jonathan, to want to rescue every vagabond you see. What's he doing up that cliff?"

I recognized one of their voices then, rich folks from two towns over, the Hansen boy, Jonathan, and his elder brother. My arms shook, my leg muscles cramped, my nose ran; there was no need for me to waste breath while I scrambled down.

A lass responded then. "From the look of those hawks winging in, he's stealing nestlings."

Jonathan replied, "Are you two blind? Arnold, she's a girl. Nell Pritchard, the best falconer in three counties."

Dang, two peregrines were coming all right. I would not get down in time. I rushed my movements, hoping against hope that I could avoid the deep scrape of talons. Ten feet, fifteen, twenty, then a rock gave way beneath my feet as the air whirred from the beating of strong wings. My chin clipped the wall, and I tasted the iron liquid of blood.

A scream from below caused me to wonder if the rock had hit any of them.

Jonathan's urgent voice interrupted my thoughts. "She's fine, Chloe, the falcon missed her. Don't scream again. It might cause her to slip."

Chloe shut up, but the other youth babbled then. "Let's get out of here. Those birds are looking for a fight. They're going to attack her again."

It would take too long for me to descend. Bollocks! I anticipated the rake of claws as I heard Jonathan's voice not ten feet below.

"Jump. I'll catch you."

Arnold gasped. "They're diving! Run!"

"Jump!"

There wasn't time to decide. I pushed away from the cliff, hoping I wouldn't regret this. As soon as I dropped, Jonathan's arms cradled me as he tore off running.

I was too startled to free myself.

I peered out between my fingers to see the peregrines thirty feet above and closing in fast. A sound like a distressed young falcon came from beneath the trees, and the birds veered, checking themselves, and pulled off their attack.

We tucked into the forest, using the thickness of the underbrush as cover.

I disentangled myself from Jonathan's arms, embarrassed by the warmth that flooded my cheeks.

The annoying Arnold approached us. "Did you hear that? That devil bird distracted the hawk."

"They're falcons," Jonathan corrected.

The lass pointed at the raven, now hopping toward us. "Is that your bird?"

"Nae, of course, nae." Mine? Mine implied ownership. There's no profit in ravens. "I'm, we're..." I frowned, trying to explain. "'Tis just till she's better."

My chest wriggled, and they all watched as I removed the now disheveled birds.

Soot looked expectantly at the fledglings, like I had brought her an exceptionally fine treat. I gathered them back up so she wouldn't misunderstand my intentions.

Arnold didn't know when to let go. "But that raven came to your aid."

I looked at the raven seeking grubs on a downed tree. I gave her a wink. Arnold didn't need to know about our tie.

Arnold and Chloe watched me suspiciously, talking between themselves as if I wasn't there.

"Is she the last Tower called?"

Jonathan's voice dripped with sarcasm, though I thought I heard relief underneath. "She's climbing rock for falcons. If she were bewitched, she isn't anymore."

"But why is she here?"

"You might ask her. She can speak for herself."

Chloe's voice carried, "Well, are you? Tower-called, that is."

I snorted, brushing myself off to hide my embarrassment. "I was."

"What do you mean?"

"I left there four days past."

There was silence.

I considered then what were they doing out here. Mayhap they were also caught by Roselyn's magic.

I checked their faces, looking for that lost gaze that had taken Will.

Three sets of eyes stared back at me. Chloe in fascination, Arnold in disdain, and Jonathan with admiration and something else. My mind twitched. Will. I turned, trying to glimpse if he lay where I had left him.

Arnold spoke again, distracting me. He was annoying in a gnatish kind of way. "Liar, no one returns from the Tower."

"Well, I did." I thought of swatting him then, contemplating the cost of that.

Arnold was clearly soft, an eldest son, with the look of someone who was his Mama's darling. Jonathan, I knew. A year past, I'd helped him nurse a sick hawk.

I took in all their faces: full bottom lips, chestnut hair combed to a shine, and broad foreheads, kin and moneyed; all of them. I felt for Jonathan. It must be a burden to have a brother that much of a sod.

Arnold continued. "You're just making that up to look important."

I simmered, my ears heating.

Their horses nickered, and Will's horses returned their greeting. The three siblings turned their heads at the sound. Will's two horses trotted into view. I answered the group's unspoken question with a shrug. "They're my brother's."

Arnold bleated like a sheep. "The horses are probably stolen.

They're crofters. No Pritchard could own something so fine."

That decided it. I hauled off and punched him. We went down in a tangle of arms and legs. Jonathan grabbed me by my shoulders, pulling me away from Arnold; nevertheless, I managed to get in one last kick for extra. Chloe's mouth opened and closed like a beached fish. Fortunately, the peregrines didn't get hurt. I transferred them to a hastily made nest in my saddlebag with the flap half closed.

Bollocks, I was muddy again. I'd need another bath.

***

Arnold's nose bloodied up; a bruise bloomed on his chin, and his fancy pleated sleeve was torn. He carried on so over his damaged shirt you would think it was fine linen or something. I looked closer, well aye, maybe it was.

Chloe looked at me, dismayed, as if I had started this. She finally shook her head, reached into a drawstring satchel, and brought out her needle.

I brightened at the sight, willing to make nice under the circumstances.

"Can ye hem a straight line?"

Her look would have curdled freshly drawn milk.

She tossed her head, unsettling the fancy grouse-feathered hat that perched upon her head. "Anyone can. My nursemaid taught me when I was five."

I shrugged, ignoring her implication. "Well, good, then." I led them over to Will, lying exhausted on the forest floor. "I have something for ye to mend."

Chapter

14

Chloe showed more guts than I gave her highborn self credit for. After an exciting lesson in needlework, and a wee dram of whiskey to clean the wound, we retired to the comfort of the fire. Will fell back asleep and didn't awake until dinner. Jonathan retraced his journey back to a copse of trees about half a mile from here, returning with small green shoots of willow. I boiled them up in some water and poured the resulting tea down Will. By late evening, his color improved, and his fever abated. Afterwards, Jonathan helped him to sit up so he could wash and shave. Without all those bristles, Will looked less hairy, but gaunt and ill.

Arnold ignored me, sitting at the fire nursing his bruise like a wounded soldier. The way he carried on about our fight, you would think no one had ever even mussed up his hair before.

Fortunately, Chloe, as dainty as her corset-waisted figure implied, wasn't completely useless and turned her hand to tending Will, unlike Arnold, who wouldn't even light a fire.

Chloe hovered over Will, engaged with his healing now that she had stitched him up. "How did he get that knife cut?"

I shrugged. "He's been too sick to tell me. Once we get back, I'm sure Da will find out. Someone is going to pay for this." I pulled out the rest of my fish from last night's dinner.

Arnold's eyes widened. "You're eating that?"

I looked at the charred fish. So maybe it was a trifle overcooked. "It's fine. I'm nae so picky that I can turn my nose up at food."

"That's not food. It's coal."

Well, wasn't he the pampered darling? Chloe's expression wasn't any more encouraging.

Jonathan took one unfathomable look, then pushed a fishing net into my hand, saying. "Here, Nell. Chloe will watch Will for you. Why don't you get us some more fish, and I'll fry them up?"

After one final check on my brother, I trotted off.

***

We sat around the fire, warming ourselves against the brisk night air. Will stirred in his sleep, calling out to Roselyn, but otherwise seemed a touch better. Jonathan dealt with the horses, coaxing them to him with his gelding. I walked down to the bank to get water.

At the stream's edge, I felt a prickle. You might think I would have turned away at that, but I was determined to fill the water skin. A swirling vapor rose above a small eddy and, before I could react, a face stared back at me—the Guardian. "Come back. Please, come back. The Tower, it's—"

I almost fell in with surprise; my water skin dropped, hit the water, and dispelled the image. Quickly, I grabbed the now-filled skin. I backed away, my heart racing and my stomach cramping from fear. We needed to leave, and soon.

When I returned, Will was awake and crawling to his knees. "She's so sad. And it's been so long." He stilled, as if listening to something far away. "I'm almost there, Roselyn." And he scrabbled forward, collapsing not three feet beyond.

Chloe and I calmed him down. After a single glance my way, she brushed the moss away that had fallen from his ears. But there were questions in their eyes after that, lots of questions. Ones I didn't want to answer.

Jonathan joined us. "Is he speaking about the Tower?"

I dragged out my answer. "Yes."

I buttoned my lips, afraid saying more aloud would give Roselyn power. Just looking at Will responding to her made me jumpy.

"Is his Roselyn trapped in there?"

I couldn't avoid speaking of it completely, not after that show. "She's the magician. The one who traps lovers."

"Is there anyone else there?"

At my hesitation, Jonathan continued. "We're seeking our sister, who disappeared a year ago."

Chloe asked, "Did you see her? Is she there?"

I must have paused a tad too long as their tension rose.

"There were pictures on the walls of those trapped. Nae one alive. Roselyn's magic claims any who venture close."

Jonathan asked, "Pictures? Was one of them blonde with a small mole on her cheek?"

I hedged. "The drawings weren't very clear."

Jonathan looked over at Chloe. "Maybe we should continue on, just to make sure…"

Roselyn would trap them in no time flat. Who knew what she might do, what kind of power she still wielded? Perhaps she would turn them into bushy-tailed squirrels or mice. They couldn't go. I knew the hazards better than anyone.

I shook my head. "It's a dangerous place. I barely escaped myself. Her magic is deadly."

I needed to get home with my brother. I couldn't turn back.

And anyway, there was no way for us to rescue them, no way to fix it, only death.

Arnold asked, "Where would we find a magician who can break this?"

I threw my hand in the air, upsetting the raven. "I'm a simple country lass, a crofter, remember? What would I know of magicians?"

Arnold needed to assert himself by putting me in my place. "I wasn't asking you, girl. We can all see what you are." I ignored his insult. We both knew he was all noise and no fight.

I turned to Jonathan and Chloe. "What was your sister's name?"

Jonathan answered. "Dulce."

My gut wrenched. Dulce, the wraith that helped me.

Fortunately, the night was upon us, so they couldn't read the knowledge in my face. Of all those trapped within the wall, why did it have to be their sister I had spoken to, made promises to?

Will stirred then, groaning, reaching out to fend off some unseen foe. I rushed to his side, happy for the distraction.

Later, later, I would tell them. But first I had to get my brother home, had to get him safe. The wraiths were no longer human. There was nothing that could be done, was there? Will was alive. Him, I could rescue.

The raven chose to speak then, croaking out an understandable, "Resist."

Bollocks. This was not the time for her to show off her language skills. I cringed at this reminder of Dulce's request as guilt wrestled with duty in my exhausted brain. Dulce wanted her brothers, and here they were.

Chloe sighed. "We hoped that miraculously she might still be alive. That perhaps you knew of the others."

I held my tongue, unwilling to lie more than I already had.

Chloe took my silence as affirmation, looking away as if I had confirmed her deepest fears. I felt for her, truly I did. I remembered how it hurt when my brother left. And this was worse, not knowing what happened at all.

But I did, and though I knew Dulce was there, I had no way of saving her. I didn't even know if the wraiths lived. And I wasn't putting these people at risk for naught.

Chloe spoke into her hands. "I miss her so. She was the eldest of us, a year older than Arnold. All we found was a gold coin left in the center of her bed. We knew then what had happened."

Was there gold exchanged for me also? Money left under my pillow like teeth. Or did Roselyn have some pecking order of how much each person was worth?

Arnold inserted his *wisdom* into this. "I knew we wouldn't find her; it's been over a year."

Chloe said something then, something that caused the skin on my arms to shiver. "Jonathan, I almost thought you might be affected by the Tower."

Jonathan busied himself feeding the fire and didn't speak.

"Jonathan?" Chloe repeated.

"Dulce is our sister. Of course, we would feel the pull," he stated as he moved the logs around on the fire.

Should I tell them? Jonathan and Chloe deserved to know. I debated. But they would die if they continued on. I knew they would.

The annoying Arnold interjected his comments again— something about his discomfort in the woods—and it pulled me back. I would tell Jonathan later once Will was safe and I figured out how to break the Tower's magic.

Arnold spoke again, perhaps wanting to assert himself as the eldest in the family. "Is it like they say? Gold stacked higher than your eyeballs?"

Arnold stood staring at me, waiting for an answer. I decided to overlook our past quarrel and answer him like he was a nice person, which he wasn't. They were helping me get Will home, after all.

"Nae, really, nothing gold. Rich things certainly, lace and silk and such, but nae gold."

I saw his eyes narrowing, disbelieving me. I sat up straighter, ready to slam him again. My temper was short with lack of sleep. He wasn't the laird here. He had no right. I readied myself as he snorted and opened his mouth, "Do you really expect us to…"

Jonathan stepped between us, speaking sharply, "That's enough, Arnold. We're not going to accomplish anything by bickering with one another."

Arnold snapped, "Well, Jonathan, aren't you the peacemaker? First you drag us out here into the wilds, no servants, no cook, and clearly, no good reason. Then you invite this uncouth chit to our fireside. All this, and we still don't have proof of what happened to Dulce. You—"

I was definitely tired of him. It was my fire, anyway. It had been a trying few months, otherwise I would never have continued being this rude to him. He could be a potential customer. My gaze whipped over to Will again to see if Arnold's voice had awakened him. He slept.

Speaking over his racket, I interrupted him. "Is he always this noisy?" I asked, turning to Jonathan and Chloe.

"Mostly," Jonathan agreed with a grin.

Arnold swelled up like a toad. "Wait 'til Mom hears that you are taking the side of a crofter against me. So much for finding out what happened to our sister." He took a breath amidst his fussing. "I bet this was just a paltry excuse to get away from Father."

Chloe sat next to my brother, her eyes welling with tears. "Leave off, Arnold. We're all tired and disappointed." Arnold's eyes snapped toward her, startled by her defection.

Jonathan looked directly at his brother. "True. Looks like I was wrong. Dulce is gone. But if we can't return with news of Dulce, let us return home with our honor intact and our kinship untainted."

Arnold seemed to take that as a concession and sniffed

disdainfully in my direction. He wasn't worth the sack to drown him in. But my heart sank knowing it was their sister locked in those panels, locked in the walls as a wraith. I was betraying her and them.

***

I did my best to ignore Arnold, busying myself with my fledglings. Jonathan and Chloe, I could barely face. But my mind couldn't let go of what I knew. I worried over what would happen to the wraith Dulce and all the others.

My brother rustled but remained asleep. I went back to my birds, fussing over them to distract myself. Chloe sewed me little rufters—eye hoods—for each of them. I cut leather into thin strips and braided them into jesses.

I sat gloating over my new nestlings, pushing off my guilt.

The large male, though sulky, tolerated me, but the female would have none of it. She fought each touch. She was large and beautifully fledged. Once she was tamed, she would be quite the prize.

Jonathan came up behind me. "May I help?"

"Um, thanks. Can ye hold him while I put the jessing on?"

Jonathan nodded.

"How is the sparrowhawk that we nursed? Is she still well?"

"That one was Arnold's. Father gave him the hawk, but he ignored it. It would never return to him. I spent many afternoons luring it back. We had one other before that, which was Dulce's, a beautiful red kite. Tame as can be."

"Does she have a vee notched in her left wing?"

He nodded. "One of yours?"

I nodded. "Aye."

"I wonder," he said. "After we return... would you help with my hawks again? Maybe teach me about hawking."

I nodded, afraid to seem too eager. Maybe he and I could be

friends? We had spent some time talking that fall. He had an easy way about him, a good disposition for hawking. Even now, my birds were calming beneath his hands.

That might have been why I had fancied him when I was a wee lass, not that he ever knew. His hands caressed my birds, and my cheeks felt like flame. Surely, I outgrew that silliness, hadn't I? I did not want to be some rich person's doxy. But friends?

Arnold called over, then, and that thought blew away. That's why I had avoided him last year. They were rich merchants, nothing in common with my folk.

The evening breeze picked up, Roselyn's voice wrapping itself within the winds. I turned my head from it, listening instead to the night sounds: frogs croaking in the pond, a lone fish making a splash, the whoosh of an owl on its rounds. My brother, exhausted from the ride and stitching, never awoke. The raven tucked her head 'neath her wing as if all was right in her world.

Jonathan and I sat around the fire watching while Chloe tried to get some rest. Arnold pulled his pallet away from us, snoring like a rooting stoat.

And I sat well into the night thinking of promises and obligations.

Chapter

15

Roselyn upped her calling the next morning. Even with his ears stuffed with moss, Will fought us, determined to respond to his love. I fought my own wars with her siren calls. Jonathan's soothing voice kept me steady. We bundled Will up, shoving him onto the yellow horse. Our bodies pressed together as we worked to get him settled. I felt myself blush at Jonathan's closeness. Arnold noticed, his mouth drawing into a tight, disapproving line.

"Jonathan," Arnold said.

"Yes?"

"Have you offered on Mabel yet? I know you visited over there last week." Arnold gave me a knowing wink. "And the week before."

"Oh yes. Looks like—"

"Well, good." Arnold turned his back on his brother. "They're like this." And he overlapped his fingers.

I stared at him like it was nothing to me that Jonathan had a lass. But even though I knew Jonathan was far beyond my station,

I felt a pang of disappointment.

***

We arrived home late that day, gathering a parade of village gawkers. No one had ever returned from the Tower. I was the first. That and my brother's appearance after seven years' gone would have been plenty of fodder for the villagers to natter about. But we pranced in traveling with wealthy folk, the Hansens: Jonathan, Chloe, and the unpleasant Arnold. Me, sporting my borrowed moth-holed pants and carrying a raven. It was epic story material. Even without me returning astride a fancy horse, it was enough to supply our hamlet with gossip for generations.

My bum hurt, and I was tired, but snugged beneath my jerkin were the two peregrines, who were already starting to tame up. The raven watched the show from the cantle of my saddle, proud as any noble.

Down the lane, the laundry fluttered for all to see: all sizes of patched boy clothes, gray-tinged woolens, small clothes, much-repaired linens and all. On the west side, under a rough thatched cover, were five posts set into the ground. Upon three sat tethered hawks: a hooded merlin, tiny and sleek; a kestrel, thin-winged with its red back to us; and a goshawk, all hunched and fierce. Da must be working feverishly to get them tamed up and ready to sell.

I pretended not to hear Arnold's snide comments as we approached, nor see Jonathan's hand motion of reproach.

Three of our dogs careened out onto the dirt path, warbling our arrival: Pepper, Fidelus, and Rowdy.

As Da limped out, trying not to favor his bad knee, the expression of pride and relief on his face made me glow. But there were many questions on his face that would need to be answered. He was followed by Mam, whose calm burst like an August seedpod when her eyes lit on Will and me.

Will lifted his head, stretching a weary smile across his face.

94

"Hi, Mam. Good to be home." He folded back into himself, his face taut with exhaustion.

Mam quickly regained her composure and organized our return. My brothers surrounded us, hailing me as a cross between a conquering hero and a ghost raised from the dead. Will was carried inside, Mam and Da glued to his side.

Our three companions kept their distance, unsure, I suspect, of how to act around ordinary folk. The raven flapped her wings and scooted across the grounds, keeping pace with me in an awkward attempt to fly.

Da returned to stand in the doorway. Hawk mules streaked his shoulders and down his shirt. He came forward to bob his head to Arnold and Jonathan. "I thank ye fer the return of my young ones. They mean everything tae me."

'Twas unfair. I started to put things to rights, but Da tightened his hand on my shoulder. The gentry like to believe in their importance. Da always said it doesn't hurt to coddle them. It never hurt sales to flatter potential buyers.

Jonathan spoke up in my defense. "This was all Nell's doing. She escaped the Tower and found her brother, not us."

I fessed up to their help. "Chloe stitched Will up, and Jonathan found the willow to break his fever. I couldn't have done it without them."

Arnold's face flushed slightly with my omission of his name. He shouldn't have hoped that I would mention him. He had sulked all the way home. No way was I giving him credit for being anything but annoying.

Da patted me on my shoulder. "Well, if anyone could hae returned from there, 'twould hae been Nell. Nae one can keep my lass from doing what she wants fer any length of time."

The crowd gathered in our yard grew buggy with interest.

Thornton, his voice rasped from too much tobacco, asked. "How did Nell escape?"

After a silence, Da answered for me, proud as a grouse during spring, "'Tis Nell, folks. Ye know her, as clever and independent a critter as any fox or badger."

"That's all well and good for you. Your girl is returned," Willum's son called out, "but what of the others who are missing, our sons and daughters? What happened to them? Should we mount another rescue?"

Another voice, one I didn't recognize with all the noise, spoke. "Those who have gone there have failed, returning dazed and broken."

"Magic requires a price. What price will we pay for Nell's escape?"

Da answered, "Dinnae go there. There's nae price. Nell's here, and naught will come o' it."

My thoughts turned to the Guardian and the wraiths, to Dulce and Roselyn, even the spider. No one could touch the Tower without being absorbed. Even with my knowledge 'twas a near thing. And that with the Guardian aiding me.

"I... 'Tis true it's a dangerous place, with magic set to grab," I said, recalling my wretched climb out: my lungs crushed, stones thrown. No one should go there. There was no hope and only Roselyn waiting, her snare set.

The noise of the crowd drowned me out. Da motioned for everyone to quiet down before gesturing for me to continue.

"Nae one should go near. 'Tisn't safe," I hedged.

Someone spoke up. "We've lost many a lad trying to breach the Tower, only to return addled and ill."

I heard an audible groan from someone in the crowd as one woman was led away sobbing, tears streaming down.

Jonathan and Chloe watched with tight faces. Remembering their sister, I supposed.

On the wind, Roselyn's voice carried. From within the house, I heard Will cry out in response. No one else appeared to hear her;

they continued talking among themselves, oblivious to the pull of that sorrowful call.

Another voice, Mary Mackell maybe from the shrill edge of it. "Nell, so how'd ye get away? Did ye fly?"

Jonathan and I exchanged glances. Where did these folks get these ideas?

"I climbed out," I said. Around me, voices murmured, not believing me.

"How high was the gold piled?"

I frowned. "What?"

"The gold, Nell. How high? How much gold did you bring back?" someone asked.

Everyone's head bent toward me, listening for my response.

"'Tis silly. There are nae stacks of gold. I brought back what was there for the taking, a broken, black raven."

Da laughed, but within the crowd, I heard whispers and scoffing.

A voice in the back called forward. "Come on, Nell. Tell us aboot the gold, the stacks of gold? How much?"

Another man followed up on this. "There must be piles of it. For every maiden that's been taken, coin is left, gold worth more than a man's month's wages."

Here it was again. I knew the Tower better than anyone alive. "Gold? There was nae gold."

"Ye must have seen something, some glint of metal stashed in a corner."

I shrugged, tired of this discussion and wanting all these people to go home.

Someone called out again. "But how'd Nell get back without her brains scrambled? What price did she pay? Or maybe she's magic herself?"

Da waved them away. "Pshaw! Nell, magic? Come now, time fer us to gan about our business. My bairns are worn from their travel, and ye, my good friends, hae work to do."

One of my least favorite neighbors, he of the long nose hairs, kept staring at my bosom. Finally, he pointed at me. "Well, gold or no gold, unless she's hiding apples down her front, looks like they fed her well." Everyone laughed.

Jonathan looked like he wished to speak with me, but I was too embarrassed. I stormed inside, my moment of glory gone. The neighbors were disbursing, anyway. The show was over. I looked out from the front window, watching Jonathan and Chloe move down the lane, surprised at my disappointment at their going.

Jonathan twisted in his saddle, looking back toward my house. I pulled back from the curtain, not wanting him to see me watching like a lovesick lass. But I couldn't help but think that his Mabel was surely getting a good fella.

I saw the yard as he must, the fence with two stakes missing, looking much like a gap-toothed six-year-old. The house needed white-washing. Flowers leapt up everywhere, Mam's hand in evidence, but nothing that would interest a merchant's son. Any wayward thoughts I might have harbored, I let go. We could never even be friends.

Eleven-year-old Ben came up behind me, shocking me out of my daydream. "What's with yer hair?"

I reached up, thinking leaves might be caught in it.

"Ye always wore it loose, flying all over the place. Now it's all plaited tightly down."

I twitched my shoulder, forcing my hand down, resisting my newly developed urge to keep it tidy. "It's nothing, just easier this way." There was no way I would confess that I had gotten used to it out of my face.

By the day's end, my brother Cam popped what remained of my bubble of pride, pointing out that all I did was climb out of the Tower. Something any one of us could have done since we were ten.

Chapter

16

I took one last peek outside to see if Jonathan and Chloe were still in view. I regretted that I hadn't said goodbye. After all they had done for Will, 'twas only polite.

Two men of the Simpsin clan slithered off down the lane, and the remaining neighbors left us none too soon afterward. Da and I placed my fledglings into an empty bird coop.

Will passed out again, safe in our front room, stretched out on a hastily rigged bed. Mam bent over, checking his forehead for fever, tucking the corners of a threadbare coverlet under his chin. She grabbed my hand as I neared and hugged me to her. Her face wiped dry, but still there were tear-streaked lines on her cheeks.

Hanging on our oak wall pegs were four violins and two mandolins. An elaborately carved maple harp was pushed into the corner—Mam's from when she was young and rich. A bodhran, stretched from the hide of the last billy-goat we had, lay up against it, its beater dangling from a cord nearby. Three sets of spoons made from the flattened ribs of sheep lay on the windowsill.

No matter how tired we were, more evenings than not would find us pulling out our instruments and playing a tune or twelve. Even the littlest of us could play the spoons by the time we could run and skip.

My mind shifted to the beautifully crafted instruments lying unused in the tower, Roselyn's tower. The initials on the violin were Da's: NP, Nathaniel Pritchard. Da had crafted that violin.

Will stirred, and I wondered, could he let Roselyn go? He had worked seven years, only to return and find her lost to him, locked into her own magic.

Four-year-old Tim stared at Will from beneath Mam's arm, in awe of this man in our front room, the older brother he had never met.

Mam raged as she fussed over Will. "Who could have done such a thing? Attack someone and leave him for dead."

Da shook his head. "There be some rough folk out there, Maura. People who ye would nae want to acknowledge as friend or family."

Mam's voice sank. "But to leave someone like that?" She shook her head in disbelief, her shift not hiding her stomach. She placed a kiss on my cheek. "Nell, you did well. All our children are here now and safe."

The boys came in then, my brothers with their boots clattering and banging, three of our dogs trotting behind.

Hal came over and patted my head like a puppy. "We thought ye were lost forever, Sis."

Ben returned from dumping the fireplace ashes. "What happened in the Tower, Nell? Were there monsters and dragons and magic? What was it like?"

Fidelus and Rowdy, our hunting dogs, growled over a bone that found its way into the house. As the dogs' tempers rose, Tim stuck his hand into that fury, getting a sound nip for his efforts.

Da grabbed our dogs and shoved them outside while Mam tried to staunch the bleeding from Tim's finger.

I loved my family, all of them, but I had forgotten how young Tim's hollers echoed in this little room. How loud all my brothers were. How hard it was to get heard over the dogs' barking and the chickens clucking and Da calling for silence over it all. Mam seemed not to notice the racket. She looked at me, expecting I'd continue talking over this fuss.

There was a space soon after when I could answer my brother's question. I picked up the bone from the floor. "Quiet," I said. "It was quiet."

No one heard me. Ben jostled Cam, who pounded him good, until Da stepped in with a booming, "Lads, quiet down." There was another breather.

Hal asked, "What did ye say, Nell?"

Cam joined in, still holding a yelling Ben in an armlock. "Yeah, Sis, what did ye do for over a month?"

The door flapped open as Ben kicked out. Fidelus and Rowdy took the opportunity to career back inside. Before I had the good sense to let go, both dogs leapt at the bone. I went down under their combined weight.

As I picked myself up, my clothes now covered in muddy dog prints, I responded, "I took baths."

Chapter

17

The next evening, Mam coaxed Will into joining us at dinner. He was still weak and drawn, but Mam wanted to chase the daze in his face, and there was no better way than to engage him with our mealtime banter. I helped him to the table.

Da cleared his throat. "Can ye nae tell us what happened, Son?"

Will startled out of his dreaming. "What?"

Da gave me a look before saying, "I asked how ye came tae harm."

Will hunched over as though remembering caused him pain. "Three men attacked me late one evening." As Will spoke, Da's hands tensed against his leather chaps. "My horses spooked and ran, but my money, three hundred ducats, and a copper-colored bull, they took." Will's head hung. "It wasn't everything Roselyn's father demanded, but I hoped that this would be enough. It's been seven years. I promised. I swore I would return for her. Now all is lost but my horses."

Da laid his roughened hand on Will's shoulder. "Son, ye are here and alive, and yer sister's back from that death trap. 'Tis more than anyone could ask fer. Certainly more than anyone could expect."

"Roselyn's waiting for me."

Da frowned and tried again. "Roselyn's gone."

Will retreated into himself. He didn't seem convinced.

Da said, "'Tis nae yer fault. She didnae wait fer ye, she didnae believe ye would return."

I kept my mouth shut. I knew why she hadn't believed. The Guardian had destroyed all the letters Will had sent her. He made sure that Roselyn had no hope of Will returning, no hope at all.

Will said nothing. He sat with that haunted look in his eyes, as if he was a hundred miles from here.

Da cleared his throat. "The men who stole from ye, dinnae ye recognize them? Anything notable? Tall, short?"

Will twitched as though startled, and then shook his head. "They were big men, not so much tall as beefy. Their faces covered." He looked down, his face still pale from the fever. "It's been so long since I was here. I'm fairly sure they weren't boys I ran with."

Da nodded. "They must be outsiders, long gone now. We would hae heard if it was anyone local. I'll ask around. A bull, copper or other, 'tis nae an easy thing tae hide."

***

The next morning, after Da returned from milking the goat, I joined him in dumping the milk into our kettle. While waiting for it to curd, we sat on the porch admiring Will's horses. I was also trying to keep track of Soot, who had climbed to the top of the dovecote and now eyed our doves like a shepherd inspecting his flock.

Da eyed the raven. "Ye had to bring a raven back, lass?"

"Aye, Da. She helped me."

He snorted; his lips pursed like he might take me to task over this. Then, in his usual laconic way, he shrugged, dismissing it as unimportant.

"Get my fiddle, will ye, lass?"

I stepped over to the wall where our instruments hung and grabbed two fiddles, Da's maple one and mine of willow.

"We hae much to be joyful about today. Just a few songs to celebrate, then back to work."

As Da tuned, one by one, my brothers spilled in. Ned and Ben arrived sweaty from working in the backfield, Cam from the chicken coop.

Will rallied enough to push himself into a half-sitting position. Tim handed him a mandolin so he could pluck the melody along with us.

My fingers rushed to tune my fiddle as Da nodded to each of us.

Mam stopped scrubbing the laundry and sat down at her harp. Tim climbed out from behind the chair and, grabbing a set of spoons, followed the beat set by Cam's bodhran. Soot clamored over to the porch window, stretching out her wings for balance. She looked like she planned on joining in with a song.

Da started playing a pretty tune, a hornpipe from when he was a lad. I stepped in with the melody. Ned and Hal sallied forth with a harmony, and Mam added trills to dress up the piece.

Two songs later, Da put down his fiddle and looked at each of us in turn. "Well played, my lads and lasses." His gaze lit on Tim, who was looking at Will's mandolin. "Tim, as soon as this harvest season is o'er, I'll build ye a mandolin. I've got the perfect wood curing now." He smiled and hung the fiddle back on the wall. "Back to work. Those fields won't plow themselves."

He started outside, then checked himself. He reached under his frayed jacket and pulled out a handful of scrunched wildflowers. "Maura, for ye, my love. For the pleasure of your company these last twenty-five or so years." He gave her a soft kiss on the cheek and limped back outside to work.

Mam didn't move. I walked over to her, and she pulled me close. "Ah, Nell, when times are hard, your father knows how to make it right. When you marry, you could do worse than look to him as a standard."

I frowned at her comment. Marry? I'd only just returned. We didn't need to start on that.

But as I walked back to the house, the wind picked up, and I heard Roselyn's voice once again.

Rose, Rose, Rose, Rose
Will I ever see thee wed?
I will marry at thy will, sire
At thy will.

I peered through the window at Will, his face turned to the wall. In the far distance, lightning flashed in the clear sky. She couldn't leave us alone, could she?

Chapter

18

Da limped onto the porch dripping sweat, his feet caked with mud. I trotted behind, pulling off my wool cloak. We sat on the rickety bench to remove our boots. Mam, her face drawn with exhaustion, bent over Will's bedside holding a bowl of broth.

"Maura." Da's voice lowered. "Ye need to sit."

"It's so little to do. I can't sit and watch all of you work."

"'Tis exactly what I want ye to do, sit. Nae more."

"But someone has to see to Will and…" she said as she carried the half-empty dish back to the kitchen.

"Nell willnae let anything happen to Will—nor will I. He's safe. All is well, my love. 'Tis ye that needs the rest. I'm nae going to hae ye run yerself into an early grave."

Mam's fingers gripped the table as her knees buckled.

Da was up and at her side in a flash. "What is it?"

"Just a twinge. It's nothing that won't pass."

"Maura, nae more excuses. Ye need to lie down."

She shook her head in denial.

"Think of the bairn."

Mam looked like she would set him up straight when her face twisted in pain.

"Maura," Da whispered, "ye need tae think of me."

Da picked her up before any of us could react. "Ned, run tae toon and get the healer. Cam, get the gold coin that was left when Nell was taken. We can pay with that."

Cam disappeared into the back room. Da gently carried Mam to the armed rocking chair with its frayed seat cover.

"Da, it's gone. A black rock is in its place."

Da's shoulders sagged as Mam laid her hand on his arm. "Nat, I'll be all right. I just need a few moments."

Will looked at me from his makeshift bed. I knew what he was thinking. The gold coin that had magically appeared when I was taken by the Tower had disappeared magically with my return.

***

The healer came and we couldn't pay. The little she did didn't seem worth the burden we now had. We owed a fee, and all she did was shake her head and say that Mam needed bed rest.

Chapter

19

Life on a croft varied with the seasons, and by even a single week later, everything had settled into its normal pattern. Well, except for the magic show that Roselyn put on each evening. The sky to the west lit up in streaks of purples and golds as her voice curled down across the winds. And a fire took out an abandoned croft that some townies mumbled was caused by tower magic.

Oh, and Mam being down. And my eldest brother having just returned. And, of course, Soot causing trouble. Other than that, it was normal. But who was I fooling? No one, not even me, though I clung to what was normal like a burr on a sheep.

We all came together for supper, the lads and Da trudging in from the fields or the barn or from working down the lane. I left the hawks after a long afternoon, passing the near pasture as I did.

Will's horses were out, cantering down the field, heads high, tails flying, then pivoting and galloping back the other way. Watching them move was a pleasure. A few days of rest, some food and water, and they were full of themselves. Da clanged the triangle, announcing that the food was ready. I waved to him and pointed at the frolicking beasts as I trotted up to the porch. Since they'd been cleaned up, they shone.

Da whistled, turning to look at Will still lying in the front room. "Look at those horses. Well, Son, ye did good fer yerself."

Will didn't respond. He sat upright there, stunned. I was a mite tired of this. As I couldn't shake Roselyn and make her leave him be, I felt near ready to shake him.

Though his wounds mended, he'd spoken no more than a few handfuls of sentences since we'd returned. My heart ached each time I looked his way.

Da's face tightened at my brother's silence, like he was expecting more. Almost as if Will heard me thinking, his eyes found mine; that passing glance that told me he regretted returning here. I wondered if he wished I hadn't rescued him.

I didn't understand, or maybe I did.

Will had done what the Guardian asked: brought back two horses, one silver and one gold, one copper-colored bull, and the money. But it was too late. Roselyn was no longer Roselyn. Not only that, but his seven years of work came to nothing, as his bull and money were stolen.

I didn't know how he could bear it.

He only stared off to the east, his head tilted, listening. I could hear her too. Keening, calling as though her heart were crushed into pieces. Will's face paled white from grief.

My hands tightened. Roselyn couldn't have my brother. Not me and not him!

Right below, her voice like a harmonic counterpoint, I remembered Dulce's voice repeating over and over, "Resist."

Six lassies and their six lads taken; did they live or were they dead, only their ghostly remains waiting to be set free? They had kith and kin who mourned, not knowing if their sons and daughters were Tower caught or had run away. No one knew for sure, no one but me.

Someone should go back, if they could be rescued, to see if there was any chance at all to save them. Someone who wouldn't get trapped, someone who knew how to climb. Someone with magic.

But no one in this township could undo magic, no one was that heroic and brave, or perhaps merely foolhardy.

Not me, of course. I had my own troubles: a dazed and damaged brother, my Mam soon to birth, and a lame Da who needed hawks finished.

Soot repeated Da's whistle, bringing me out of my thoughts. She then croaked out a clearly spoken, "*Resist.*"

Da's eyes narrowed. "What's with the raven?"

Why hadn't she picked some other word to learn? Why that one?

Our sheepdog, Pepper, bounded up to me, wagging his tail and barking at Soot.

Nonplussed, Soot let out a startling, deep, "Ruff, ruff."

Pepper's mouth dropped open, and he backed carefully off the porch, watching Soot with every step.

Perhaps she wasn't a one-word wonder.

Da's forehead wrinkled. "Cannie bird. Maybe he's too cannie."

I automatically corrected him. "She's a her."

Cam replied, 'Yah, but what good is it? What's Sis doing with a raven? We can't sell it, can't eat it. 'Tis a trash bird. Not worth the price of its feathers for quills."

I blurted out, "She's a friend," then bristled at the laughter that followed. Ben hooted and Cam stamped his feet. I should have known better.

Mam rose with an effort, looking every inch seven months gone. "Now, boys, none of your teasing. We just got Nell back. Leave her be."

Cam shut up and sent a look over at Ben to gag it.

Then he twisted his lips as if something had just occurred to him. "Nell, there is talk about in town. Word is that there's money to be had in the Tower, gold lying around for the taking."

I rolled my eyes. "They've been saying that forever. 'Tisn't true."

"Aye, but some think ye know how to get in. That ye have protection from the Tower's magic."

Everyone waited for my response.

Ben slammed our door closed as if determined to prove that he could batter it down and Tim let out a howl as his finger was pinched between the door and the jamb. Mam kissed Tim's finger, and Da yelled again for Ben to be careful.

Once there was a smidgeon of silence, I answered. "It's as I said, there was nae money, nae coins, nothing. I barely escaped."

I watched the nodding of heads. Will wouldn't look my way; too torn up about Roselyn, I guessed.

"I'm nae magic. I'm just me, Nell, an ordinary lass."

Mam spoke to all of us. "Don't ever go near there, any of you. Especially you, Nell. I can't have this happen again."

Da turned to Mam. "Naebody is going there. Nae one is going to be hurt. Nell's too cannie to get trapped in a snare that she knows about. She's a sensible lass."

He looked over at Will. "Will understands that his Roselyn is gone. He's a man grown. The rest of ye need to douse these rumors. 'Tisn't healthy. There be folk who might be swayed by this talk."

Will closed his eyes like he was asleep, but I didn't believe it.

Da stood up, glancing out the window as the sun dipped lower. "Nell, first thing tomorrow morning, put Will's horses in the side pasture with the sheep. Now that they're rested, let's keep them moving. I don't want those creatures tae founder. Take Pepper with ye." The sheep dog's ears perked at hearing his name. "The ram has been feeling lively lately, and I dinnae put it past him to challenge ye."

Soot croaked out another "Resist" and then didn't take her own advice. She dove for the remaining piece of toast as Tim reached for it.

She choked it down and hopped away, letting out a raucous laugh.

Da looked at the bird as if seeing her for the first time. He wasn't pleased.

"And dae something with that bird."

I got up and grabbed Soot—no, I amended to myself, *the* raven—and gave her a shove out the window.

I took a dishcloth and laid it across my lap before picking up my fork and starting to eat.

Cam bent over the kitchen table. "Well, Sis, aren't ye the la-de-da. Look." He snatched Mam's dishtowel and made a great show of daintily wiping his chin, and then, with a great honking sound, blew his nose.

Ben picked up the refrain. "Nell's a la-de-da. Nell's a *Lady*."

"Say that again," I challenged.

He didn't need to. Ben flicked a cloth at me, snapping my chin. I chased him around the table. My father's voice bellowed after me. "Whenever ye youngsters are finished with yer morning ritual of tormenting one another, get busy and get yer chores done. Ye know yer Mam's breeding. I'll nae have ye making it harder fer her."

Mam grabbed Ben's elbow as he dashed past, putting her swollen body between me and him.

"Ben, that's enough. Here, take that cloth outside and put it in the laundry tub, and Cam, stop teasing yer sister. It wouldn't be such a bad thing for ye boys to pick up some manners."

Da intervened then, coaxing Mam to his side. "Maura, sit next tae me, my love. Don't let our rowdy offspring put ye out of sorts." He continued eating, interlocking his free hand with hers.

Cam growled. "Lady Nell might break a nail or two."

"Leave off, ye bugger," I replied.

"Look at her. All spit polished and groomed like for a Friday night ceilidh."

Da glanced up over his coney stew, his left hand clasped over Mam's. "Nell's fine."

He dug back into his supper. "As long as she can still climb up to an aerie and train a hawk, she can paint her nails red and eat from a fancy decorated dish for all I care. In fact," he looked me over, considering, "Maybe 'tis an advantage. There's nothing like a pretty face to help sell at Fair."

I blushed.

Through the open door, Roselyn's voice called to Will. Our eyes met, and his slid away into the glaze he got whenever he heard her. Bollocks and bloody bollocks. Roselyn didn't give up easily. I felt tense as a tick as I watched Will struggle against her call. Please, Will, don't listen, I silently begged.

Da continued on as though he didn't hear her. "Will, 'tis good tae hae ye back, Son. The Harvest festival's nae the same without yer fiddle playing."

Will stiffened as Roselyn's voice rose in desperation. A look of joy flittered over his face. Our eyes met; he jerked out of his daydream. I watched in horror as his expression wiped itself bare, then was replaced by despair. His hands, which had opened with longing, now clenched into fists.

Now that he was up and about, what if he left again? What if *she* called and he couldn't resist? How could I protect him now? I bit my lip so hard I tasted blood.

Da didn't seem to notice. "Once you're healed up, ye might take a look at that black-faced ewe. Last year, she had triplets, and we lost two of them tae…" Da frowned and walked over to Will. He waved his hand across Will's eyes. "Maura, what's wrong with that boy?"

"It's Roselyn, Da. She's calling him."

Da stopped and listened. "I dinnae hear anything unusual, just the normal squawks and fussing from the critters." He walked to the open window.

I joined him there. "Can ye nae hear her? The sadness in her voice, the heartbreak."

"Nell, are ye sure?"

I nodded. Da tapped his fingers against the windowsill.

Hal said, "'Tis the wind. Just the wind rustling the trees, Nell."

Da looked at me, contemplating.

"Mam?"

"Nell, I don't hear it either." But her eyes were fearful. She believed me.

If they couldn't hear her, then only two were her quarry, me and Will, and I knew better than to go. I stared at Will. I wouldn't lose him again, not this way, not to magic.

Chapter

20

Visitors seemed to grow as fast as the weeds in our vegetable garden. Our lane crawled with young men asking after my hawks or with questions about the Tower or to ask after my brother. Archie and the Wilson boys kept coming around. Even Harvey Tourney showed up. You'd think they would have better things to do.

I wasn't much for socializing with them, as I was out of sorts. At every clatter of hoofbeats, I found myself looking for Jonathan. When he didn't appear, I was miffed at myself. I knew there was no reason for him to come this way. Guilt lodged in my gut. I feared he would come, and I feared he wouldn't. Over and over, I questioned myself. Did I do the right thing keeping Dulce's fate secret? And if Jonathan knew, would he hate me forever?

I sighed, as I carried in a load of firewood, mentally throttling myself for being so stupid. Why would he bother with the likes of me? Besides, there was no time to waste dreaming. As I stacked the wood next to the hearth, Mam came in from the garden, her basket laden with over-wintered leeks and turnips. I grabbed them from her, easing her back into the house with the reminder, yet again, of what Da had said.

We were all tired. The jobs wouldn't get done if I counted petals, chewed my nails, or watched clouds go by.

I stepped back outside to feel the sun on my shoulders, checking the goat pen as I walked. They were forever escaping or getting their heads caught in the fencing. A vapor swirled above the goat trough, enveloping me.

"Child!"

How did he always know when I was alone? Even though I tried to resist, I peered into the half-filled trough at the Guardian's face. He appeared to be long without sleep; his eyes were red, his face drawn and sad.

"Go away! Leave me be. And make Roselyn leave Will alone!" I yelled.

He closed his eyes for a moment before he pleaded, "I need help. More have come. She's sending them back addled. Their minds twisted."

"Nothing to dae with me."

His voice trembled. "She's draining her magic trying to reach him. The Tower walls are cracking. Yesterday, she created a storm, and trees exploded. Birds fell from the sky. You must come back here. Else…" I threw a bucket into the water, shattering his face. I wouldn't hear another word.

Still, no matter how much I tried to prevent it, my thoughts squirreled back to Dulce and the debt I owed.

I reminded myself again and again that the Tower's troubles were not mine. So many things were unsettled. Mam sick, Da worried, Will healing. And money, always the problem of not enough coin. And though I fretted about Dulce, Will was my brother and called by Roselyn. I half hoped the whole Tower *would* sink into the earth. He had to stay safe.

116

I was out flying the merlin when I felt sure someone watched. Soot called out an alarm, and I looked to see who approached. No one. A feeling crept down my neck. I stared into the forest, wondering what she had heard. Deer, maybe? A boar? A passing neighbor not wanting to disturb my work? I squinted, wondering if that was a glint of metal in the distance or light bouncing off a deer horn.

Nothing. Whatever it was had vanished, but Soot screamed alarm again. I picked up a stout stick, just in case.

Above, I heard the screeching of my hawk, and I held up my free arm. He landed with a solid thud on my leather-covered forearm, a dove clutched in his talons. After feeding him a chunk of coney from my bait bag, I replaced his hood, set him on his perch, and walked back toward the house, feeling silly for my imaginings.

Chapter

21

The raven proved more trouble than any bird I'd ever had. Though she still couldn't fly far, she made the most of the short distances she could glide, tormenting Pepper and the other dogs, chasing our barn cat. Any food left unprotected was fair game for her; that's how she seemed to see it, a game, and she, the triumphant winner.

While it was maddening, I was intrigued by her cleverness. Whenever I had a spare moment, I set up riddles for her to solve: string that, when pulled, would give her a treat, a knotted piece of twine that led to a choice piece of meat. I would cache bits of food, little lures she could not resist. She would sit on a post watching anything but that—pretending they weren't of any interest to her.

The next day, they would be gone. The string pulled and the twine untied. She would have figured it out.

I was initially pleased.

There was a wee downside. Once I strung up my hawk bells, only to find them dragged out across the yard the next day. I would hear her raucous laughter as she stole food from my brothers. Tim, at four, was her favorite, an easy victim.

I returned from the millers to find the coneys loose, overrunning our garden, a quarter of the seedlings eaten.

The raven had unlocked their cages.

Da came up behind me and stared over at the destruction in Ma's garden. He knew. He settled his cap back on his head before helping me corner all four coneys. When we finished, he pointed up to Soot supervising from the pine tree. "Wring her neck and be done with it."

Da's face told me he meant those words, and I knew I should obey him. We couldn't afford her mischief.

But I couldn't bring myself to kill her. We had a bond, a common experience. I pleaded, and Da softened. Soot got a reprieve, a day and then another week. But I knew it couldn't last. Da was right. She was a wild thing and wasn't useful in any way. We didn't have the money for a pet, a destructive one at that.

***

Late spring drew its wonder across the countryside, bringing with it rain, flowers, and births. Creeks were now burbling with water, the ground moist and fertile. In our pasture, the ewes lambed, down-robed chicks, goslings, and ducklings hatched. We were awash in babies.

We'd been home but two weeks. Will's cut mended. He seemed better, though he would gaze out across the wildflower-covered hills when he thought we didn't see. Mostly he settled in, turning a quiet hand to whatever tasks needed doing, barely acknowledging the giggling lassies who flicked their skirts at him when they walked by on their way to the fields.

To all but the most keen observer, my brother was healed. He helped me when our kestrel escaped, spending a half-day tracking that bird through brambles and gorse until it surrendered to its

120

stomach and flew to our lure. Each day he'd gained strength until now he was up most of the day.

Will had returned, and that's the way I planned to keep it. His fiddle playing joined with Da's each night, making our small house sing with their harmonies. But when evening fell, Roselyn's calls set my teeth on edge, and I would seek him out. I would not lose my brother again.

I made sure I passed him by as I headed for my birds. He was across the far pasture, working his horses with long reins, preparing them to pull a cart. Even out in the field, I could see the sorrow in the set of his back as he walked steadily behind those horses. He spied me and raised his hand in a casual salute. I kept my eyes on him; I knew he wasn't over Roselyn. I sauntered over and gave him a quick hug.

"Dinnae work too hard, Will. You're still healing."

He nodded. "Work's good for me. I'm fine, Sis. I'll take a shuteye before dinner."

After feeding the goats and shoveling manure, I grabbed a few minutes to work the peregrines. They were coming along beautifully. I could hear the chink of coin every time I handled one.

Far in the distance, my raven sat lodged at the top of the weathervane, watching her world. From her vantage point, Soot saw him first, calling out, "Resist," long before Jonathan hailed me. As I tethered my birds, my heart wouldn't stop hammering. He dismounted and came over. I tried to hide both my joy and my guilt from him as he approached.

"Hey, Nell."

"Hey."

He fiddled with the reins before speaking again. "Thought I should come by and see how your brother was faring."

"Will's better. The cut has healed, the fever's gone. But…"

"But what?"

"There is nae life in him. He yearns for Roselyn. She calls to him every gloaming just as the sun sets. At night, I see the pain in his eyes. I can hear her too."

He made a show of adjusting the leather cinch on his mare's girth, keeping his back to me.

"Dae ye believe me?"

He nodded. "I've heard her."

My mouth dropped open. "When?"

He remained facing away, stroking his mare's withers.

He half-turned, chancing a look at me. "When you were locked within the Tower."

We both looked away. I shied away from responding. Only those who loved or those who loved someone in the Tower were called. Was it his sister? But that didn't make sense. Dulce had someone in her panel.

I wavered on whether to ask him more or change the subject—I changed the subject.

"So, what brings ye by our way? Out exercising your horse?"

He gave me this look, like I was slow. "I'm the youngest in the family, as you know. Not much in the way of prospects from there. Grandfather was a wealthy man, with a taste for fast horses, gambling, and wine."

I wasn't listening as well as I should. I kept mulling about that Jonathan had heard Roselyn's calls. But I couldn't bring myself to question him. I couldn't even bring myself to ask after his lady friend, Mabel.

Jonathan continued like this was a speech he had practiced. "He blew through his wealth like dandelion fluff in the wind. Fortunately for Grandmama, he died early, though not early enough. He left nothing but the business, some land, a small son, and a mass of debt. My grandmama picked herself up and ran the business for twenty-five years. She built it up to what it is now."

I herded my thoughts together enough to ask a reasonable question. "I thought your Da ran everything."

Jonathan snorted. "Oh, they let Dad *think* he's in charge. He's much like Arnold. He needs to believe in his importance. Grandmama keeps him busy so he doesn't step all over her and my mother's work. He gets a set allowance, which he spends in the clubs telling all how important he is."

I grinned. "So are ye planning on following in your father's footsteps or your mother's?"

"Neither. Arnold can have Dad's job. He's the chosen one. Dad tells him how essential he will be to the business. They both believe it.

"Dulce was to follow Mom, but now Chloe is being groomed for the business. I've been building up our land and find that it suits me well. I like overseeing the tenants, managing the pastures and dales. We've increased our profit off our sheep and cattle these last two years by twelve percent."

I said nothing. I always knew he was clever.

"So, would you mind if I came by again, maybe later this week?"

I felt a shiver of something unexpected—pleasure, hope, wishfulness? What was he saying? It almost sounded like courting language, but that wasn't possible. We were too far apart in standing, in land, in everything. And he had a lady.

At my hesitation, he added, "To learn how to work hawks."

"Aye, aye. That would be good." Both of us ducked our heads as though this was only a casual conversation, which it was. Nothing more.

He left with a friendly wave, cantering off down the road.

I watched, letting my thoughts fly up and roost upon a cloud for a moment. Then I looked down at my re-sewn dress and my patched hose and realized it was but a silly daydream.

When I came back to myself, what with Jonathan and my birds, I had been out longer than I'd planned.

Something nagged at me. The faintest of sobs drifted across the wind—

Will I ever see thee wed?

***

At thy will.

Roselyn. I comforted myself that Will was safe inside, sleeping.
Cam clanged our dinner triangle.

It was past gloaming. Mam sat with her head down on the
railing. In front of her was a basket of eggs, and half of them were
carefully pecked open. I knew without anyone speaking what had
happened, who the villain was.

Da had his hands crossed over his chest. This was it. No more
chances.

He sighed. "Sorry, Nell. Get that raven and kill it."

The raven would have to go now; I'd take her out to the
chopping block and end it. No matter how much I wished it were
otherwise, she was a calamity of a bird. I wondered where she was.
She had fled the scene of her crime.

My eyes filled, and I looked around for Will. He knew what she
meant to me. Roselyn's evening whine grew. It had been annoying
me like a buzzing gnat the last while.

"Where's Will?"

Mam barely lifted her head. "Taking a nap before dinner."

Da handed me the hatchet. "Nell, nae more distractions, dae it
now. Be done with it, lass."

I looked at it and steeled myself to this deed.

I shoved the hatchet into its sheath and slowly walked into our
front room. I wanted a word with Will before I killed Soot, wanted
him to pull me into a hug that meant he understood.

The brown woolen blanket was thrown back. Will's boots were
gone. I felt the creep of something bad. Maybe he went out to wash
for dinner.

"Mam, he's not here."

"Will?" She peered through the doorway. "He was asleep last I checked."

His brown leather traveling satchel was gone, not at the end of the pallet where it had lain since we returned.

"Will!" I ran to the front door.

Da and Hal turned at my call.

"What's the ruckus about, Nell?"

"Will's satchel's nae here, and I dinnae see Will."

Da guessed right away. "Hal, go check if his horses are here."

Hal called to us as we searched out back. "They're here." He must have seen my look then, as he tried to reassure me. "Nell, he would nae leave without these beauties. Nae if he was in his own mind."

A chill ran up my spine. What if he wasn't in his own mind? What if Roselyn controlled him? I listened for her voice. There it was, but the tone had changed—a pleased cooing.

I flew down the dusty road. Da limped after me. As we passed the lower paddock, both of us stood unmoving while we watched. Will was down the lane, surrounded by a thick mist. Soot launched herself at Will, legs extended, flying at him. He must have left with little thought, as he was on foot. Will held his hands up to protect his face, backing up step by step. The raven, my raven, was driving him home, herding him like a sheepdog with swoops and dives. Ned got to Will first, grabbing his shoulders and shaking him. From within the mist, I heard a wail—Roslyn. Will's eyes blinked rapidly as he looked around. He covered his head with his arms as Ned led him back to the house. Far away, Roselyn's voice shattered, the sobbing restarted. My teeth ached with the yearning.

Da watched, looking at Will, then at Soot, now preening on a fence post, and then at me. "Ye can put away the hatchet, Nell. Maybe we can keep that bird another day or so."

From out of a clear sky, lightning struck a copse of elm trees, and branches crashed to the ground. Fidelus, Rowdy, and Pepper raced out, barking fiercely, looking for the enemy. Cam and I grabbed buckets of water to douse a small fire smoldering in a clump of downed grass.

Finally, the sun set, and the night wind blew Roselyn's voice away.

Chapter

22

Roselyn and my struggle over Will got pushed to the sideline the next day. Yes, she continued her wailing every twilight, and Will sorrowed more and more, but I stood on the edge of a potentially more dangerous pit than even the Tower.

Da walked in, mopping his brow before placing a kiss on Mam's cheek and a pat on my back. He grabbed a slice of bread, a hunk of cheese, a boiled egg, and some pickled onion. After measuring out a handful of mint and chamomile leaves into two mugs, he removed the kettle from its place over the hearth and poured in water.

Mam spoke. "Bess agreed to come for my laying in."

I groaned and carried my plate to the metal bucket to scour it clean.

Da shuffled his feet, the only indication that he wasn't pleased. I agreed; six weeks with Mam's rich younger sister—none of us would survive it. Last time she graced our house was a single afternoon two years' past, dripping with jewels and snobbery, barely setting foot across our threshold for an hour. Even Da, who thought well of everyone, blessed the moment she left.

Mam said, "She can share Nell's bed, give Nell a chance to bond with her aunt."

I wasn't having any of this. "I'm nae sharing with her. I'll sleep on the back porch."

Mam ignored me, looking at Da.

Da found his voice, conceding, "'Twill comfort me tae know that someone is here with ye while Nell and I are at the fair next month."

But Da's look implied he would prefer anyone but Aunt Bess to come.

This must be serious if Mam considered Aunt Bess a help. She hadn't darkened our doors for any span of time since Tim's birth.

Mam sat on a stool, prepping the parsnips. A long coil of peelings for the chickens emerged from beneath her hands. She watched us both, looking like she was getting ready to explain.

Da handed Ma her mug, then deftly switched the subject, repeating his litany, "Maura, yer tae rest."

Mam snorted. "This isn't work. I find it relaxing."

Da and I exchanged glances.

Mam flicked her gaze my way before she spoke next. "Ned is planning on offering for Mary McPearson this summer. It will be a little tight, but our Nell will start her own household soon and be moving on."

What? I stopped mid-scrub and turned to Da.

Da's eyebrows lifted then, as had mine. He scraped his leavings into the pail, giving Mam a squeeze as he passed. "She's but a bairn, Maura. Dinnae rush my lass out of the house fer convenience's sake."

"Your 'lass' has grown up. Look at her." I stopped drying the dishes, wondering what her point was. "She's put on weight and gotten some curves. Didn't you notice the Wilson boy staring at her? He came by three times this past fortnight."

I protested. "He wanted to see how my hawks were coming along."

"It wasn't the hawks he was admiring."

Da scowled but kept his peace.

I tried to joke my way past this. "Mam, I just returned. Ye trying to get rid of me?"

She looked at me with sympathy. "You know me better than that. Your time in that Tower changed you. You're different. There's a look about you, a mystery, an allure. Something other than just filling in with a little weight. You speak differently. Even the neighbors noticed." Mam turned. "Tim, get out from under the table. Nell, help him get his trousers buttoned, will you, dear?"

I snatched Tim before he scooted by me. While tidying him up, I looked at Da to reason with her.

He tried tossing out a sensible objection. "Yer hands are full enough, Maura, ye dinnae need tae put more on yer plate than yer own health and our new bairn."

Mam shook her head. "Nat, Nell's almost sixteen. We need to look to her future. It won't take much to put out the word that we've a marriageable daughter."

I listened in growing alarm.

Da brushed aside Mam's words. "There's nae need tae rush this. It can wait a year or three."

Mam pinned Da with a single look. "You're putting this off, Nat. It's going to happen someday, and that day is coming soon."

"Come, Maura, our Nell's special. We cannae hand her o'er to any lad that's feeling his oats."

Mam raised an eyebrow at Da, and he grinned before wiping it from his face.

"Maybe I can talk Bess into taking Nell in hand. She could introduce her to more affluent suitors. How about that merchant boy that you came back with? Arnold, wasn't it?"

My eyes widened at the thought. Now there was a disaster worth avoiding, Arnold and Aunt Bess at the same time.

Mam trudged on, not letting up on this subject. "Or perhaps the younger brother, Jonathan, is a better match." Mam looked over at me, assessing. "I saw him stop by last week."

Da interceded before I stepped in it with both feet.

"They're rich merchants, she wouldnae know what tae dae with herself as somebody's city wife. Nell's a falconer. The best around."

Mam wouldn't be put off. "That's what makes her value even more. She's pretty, healthy, and she can read and do sums. There is no one in two hundred miles better at training raptors. Many families would want her."

"Nell dinnae want tae be some fancy, well-heeled woman who sits around serving tea." He looked at me, a small pain crossing his face. "Dae ye, lass? She's a country girl. Besides, Maura, they turned their backs on ye when we married."

Mam shook her head. "It's time, past time, for us to let go of that. The boys can make their way here, but Nell needs a home and security."

Da's face fell as if this were directed at him, at his ability to provide for us.

This was not good. Da was weakening before Mam's determined onslaught. "Da!" I wailed.

Da pulled himself together. "We can think about this after this coming fair." He winked at me. "There be plenty of time tae rid ourselves of one scrawny brown-haired lass. We hae too many hawks to train and market." He tweaked his shoulders like that settled the subject.

Mam wasn't having this. "That is my point. She *isn't* a child anymore. The two of you aren't going to turn me with your banter. You can't keep her here forever."

Da answered with a noncommittal grunt.

Mam gave him a stare. "Maybe we should look at the Simpsins

two towns over. I hear they are making money hand over fist. Someone said they just bought a carriage."

Da got a funny look on his face. "Hear tell they got a black bull they've been putting up fer stud."

He gave me a knowing look, as he tugged a small copper coin from his pouch. He casually rubbed off the black tarnish with his fingernail. Ah. Da wondered as I did about their new prize animal. Will's copper bull stolen, and a copper coat could be turned black.

Mam continued unaware. "What's their eldest boy's name again? We should consider him also."

Da sipped his tea as if considering what he would say next. "Angus. His name is Angus. I think nae him."

I was all wrapped up thinking on black dye and bulls when Mam slammed her palms on the table and rose. "Then whom, Nat?"

Da frowned and held out his hands, conceding. I saw the look she gave him. He scrunched his shoulders and buried his head into his tea. We both knew when to give way to Mam.

She remained silent, sitting down carefully. I kept quiet in the futile hope this might still blow over. I knew that in her mind the subject was done and sealed.

She spoke up again. "At the very least, Bess can help Nell get her trousseau together." Mam's words landed with the finality of the executioner's axe.

Mam got up again, holding her body stiffly, and walked outside. I followed her out to the garden, sprawling down next to her as she checked the spring peas marching up the twine. I pulled weeds as we inched between rows of young plants.

Mam put her arm over her stomach. "Nell, look around you. We don't have much. What if something happened to your Da or to me?" She looked out toward town. "And I'm hoping once you're promised, it will put an end to the rumors in town. They frighten me."

My eye widened, but I didn't ask. It had to be about the Tower. Everyone was fussing about that too much. It was over, done.

She touched my cheek. "I want reassurance that you are settled and cared for."

I hunched my shoulders, unwilling to make any promises.

"You have changed." She took my hand and gave it a squeeze. "But only for the better, Nell."

I walked inside. Mam nailed it. I was no longer who I had been. But it wasn't better. Now I was neither fish nor fowl. Who did I want to be? I found myself unable to answer, even to myself.

Da remained seated at the table, looking off toward town. I leaned against him grateful for his solid comfort, his cheerful nature.

Da stretched his arm around me. "Our world is turning, lass. Nae one likes it. But yer Mam's right. One day we hae tae send ye off. But let's make sure that it's tae someone who will love ye almost as much as we do."

Chapter

23

I'd been sitting out on the back steps plucking doves when Da called my name. The serious timbre of his voice caught my attention, and I scurried to the house front, still covered in feathers and blood. The dogs trailed along, eager for the scraps they were sure I would toss.

A pewter-colored carriage drawn by two matched bays stood in our lane, the curtains drawn tight, a gnarled hand holding the edge of the door. Except for the beringed fingers, I might have believed no one was inside. Seemed like I stood there for a time with Da's hand patting my back like a sheep he needed to settle.

A young footman, in a fitted indigo-ribboned jacket, jumped down and opened the carriage door, revealing a small woman dressed in a velvet gown of smoky grey. It looked so inviting I held my hands together to prevent myself from petting it.

Beside me, Da tipped his tam in acknowledgement. I

fumbled a curtsy in my patched work dress.

Dame Hansen watched me for some time, and I fidgeted beneath her gaze.

"So you're the one," she said. There was a long silence while she and I stared at each other. I dropped my head. In the distance, a pied wagtail called with its sharp three-beat song.

"Jonathan speaks highly of you."

Even without her mention of Jonathan, I knew who she was the minute I saw the carriage. I'd seen it barreling along the few times I went to town. Everyone knew it was from their estate.

"My grandchildren informed me that you were locked inside the rapture of the Tower."

I nodded slowly; that was as good of an explanation as any.

"And that you escaped."

I nodded again. All my wise-mouthed talk vanished into the air.

"I'm here to settle something, something that has tickled my mind since my grandchildren returned."

I tilted my head. My chin wavered as I conjured all the things she might ask about.

"Do you know what happened to those who disappeared?"

My tongue stuck in my mouth, and I had trouble forming a sentence.

"Um…"

Her eyes seemed to bore into me. My heart pounded, banging around my chest.

"Yes?" she prompted.

I nodded a yes, unable to speak words to make her understand.

"And my granddaughter, Dulce? Did you see signs of her?"

I nodded again, certain of the guilt that must shine in my countenance.

Her face didn't change, but the light in her eyes seemed to

sharpen.

"Is she alive?" The blunt question hit me like a blacksmith's hammer, one I had asked myself many times.

I couldn't speak, almost couldn't breathe. Da watched me, puzzled by my continued silence.

She tilted her head. "How difficult a question is this? You don't seem addle-pated. She's either dead or she's not. Which is it?"

She seemed content to wait me out. Bollocks.

"Both."

She noticed Da then and made a decision. "Mr. Pritchard, would it be possible to have a private discussion with your daughter?"

Da checked my eyes. He seemed reassured by what he saw there, before he stepped away. "I'll be o'er the fence, digging out briars, Nell. If ye need me, I'll be right there."

She leaned forward. "Time for some straight talk, Nell. You're a pretty child, but you are lying. No one can be both dead and not dead." Her eyes bored into me.

"It's nae that simple."

She patted the carriage bench, inviting me to sit.

"Tell me. I'll listen."

And she fell quiet.

I told her then, sat by her side and poured out the whole story, like a floodgate opened on a levee. I told her of the wraiths, of the dangers, of my fears, and what Dulce had said. I told her about Roselyn and her magic.

Her eyes never left mine. I was surprised at the relief I felt at telling someone.

She was too proud for tears, but her eyes glistened with a sheen of sorrow she refused to let fall. "So, are you a magic talisman, as some tell?"

My mouth dropped open. How could people still be saying

this? "Me, nae. I'm just a wee lass."

She nodded like she agreed. "We need magic to fight this. But where do we get it?"

Chapter

24

Bess sparkled into our home with her gold rings and silver earbobs, raising a dust of disdain as she nosed about the house. Each of us bore her presence in our own way.

Da kept very busy. Ned helped over at the Seawald farm. Hal hid himself out in the farthest fields, not returning until late at night and falling into bed. Cam rose before dawn, dutifully prepared our breakfast, then disappeared into the barn before Bess even took off her eye shields or put on her layer of fancy makeup. Ben sought protection at Da's side like a lone sheep singled out from the flock.

Four-year-old Tim wandered the house like a ghost, banished from Mam's side by the over-protective Bess. Will took pity on him, letting him trail along trip after trip, as Will harnessed up his horses and hauled supplies in for our neighbors.

I was stuck. The only female and, as such, a command performance was required by Aunt Bess, Elizabeth Neelie, same as my name.

She sprouted a sense of superiority like feathers, her nose in the air. Much powdered and manicured, she minced through the house like a great yellow wasp. Her corset boning laced so tightly I was amazed she could walk. "Eight children in *this* house, Maura? Momma told you this would be your lot when you married beneath you."

Mam didn't respond, but a quiet smile crossed her lips once Bess turned away. Mam placed her fingers on the plain silver ring on her left hand, and a light brightened her eyes. Then she shifted the subject to one I hoped would go away. "Bess, Nell's almost sixteen. Would you take her on? I know of no hands more capable to put her marriage prospects into."

Bess and my eyes met, mine in disgust, and Aunt Bess weighing up my flaws. Her eyes flickered over me like I was some insect that crawled into her bed, evaluating if I should be crushed or not.

"Perhaps something could be made of her."

Bollocks. I'd hoped she saw me as too far gone.

Mam jollied her along, "No one could do it better. You're so much more capable at such than I."

This was not going well. I gathered myself up, preparing to make a run for it.

"Stay, child. Turn around."

I looked at Mam to see if this was to be borne or not. There was no escape. I sighed and slouched forward. Bess had me pirouette twice amidst much tsking.

Finally, she pronounced, "Well, her skin's too dark, her hands are chapped, but she has a pretty face and a decent figure; an uncut stone just waiting to be polished into a... a polished stone," she declared. Mam turned her head, ignoring the slight to me as Bess's eyes assessed me again. "Well, maybe there is some promise; she has my hair and your lips. Her waist could do with a nip, and her posture is hopeless, but a little corseting will remedy that. It will be a challenge, but we shall see what can be done." Her eyes traveled up and down me again, cataloging my defects.

Mam watched me, a cautionary look in her eyes. I bit my tongue to avoid saying something to Aunt Bess that would embarrass Mam.

After dinner, as evening settled and our lamplight shone upon our front room, I found myself seated alone beside Aunt Bess, wielding a needle and thimble, attacking a harmless piece of linen. She inspected it, and her look left little room for interpretation.

"You must be a throwback on your father's side. Maura always sewed the nicest seam, such tiny stitches and so straight. Momma expected her to make the best marriage. But she eloped with that man."

I bristled. "You mean Da."

She sniffed. "Yes, him."

It was impossible to miss Bess's disdain. I wanted to put her in her place, but I jabbed my middle finger with the embroidery needle. Aunt Bess didn't notice. She stared at the row of boy boots lined up at our doorsill. I sucked on the droplets of blood before they ruined the fine linen and I was forced to start anew.

"It's interesting how it worked out, your mother here with— Nat, and me with George. It wasn't what Mamma expected. Maura was always so quiet. We never guessed she would run off like that." She tinkled a laugh. "She didn't even confide in me."

As I inched over to grab a rag and dab it across my hand, Bess continued reminiscing, "After Maura eloped, my George was a pillar of strength. A comfort to Mama.

"I think some were surprised when George courted me and asked for my hand. They all assumed it was Maura he was partial to. She was my elder by a year, and I was not quite sixteen when he proposed. Just about your age."

Fidelus tried to nose his way into the house, and I shooed him back out, accidentally stabbing myself again while doing it.

"What happened to him?" I knew Aunt Bess was widowed young, but neither Da nor Mam ever spoke of her husband.

Bess dabbed her eyes. "I lost him early. He was such a good man. He died before his time. He was only fifty-five."

I felt a sudden sorrow for her. I couldn't imagine what Mam would do without Da.

Bess's powdered cheeks looked like the rose light of early dawn, her mouth colored like the red cowslips out in the meadow. She was beautiful. Like a porcelain doll I had once seen in a storefront, something fragile and useless but so pretty that you wanted it anyway.

"How old was he when you wed?"

"Fifty."

At my dropped jaw, her face tightened. "He was a very young fifty, quite hale. Mamma thought the world of him. She couldn't bear that both her daughters marry…" She looked at me through lowered lashes. "Mamma wanted me to do *well*," she amended.

I gritted my teeth; there was always a dig at my Da. Bess and her marriage at sixteen to a rich old man when Mam had run off with Da, young, handsome, and poor—a luthier and musician. My fingers now likened to a pincushion, needle-stuck fifteen times in the past hour.

Mam moved slowly in from the back room, looking from one to the other of us suspiciously. "Well, Bess, how are you and my Nell getting along?"

Bess's laughter tinkled like a goat bell. "Lovely. Just sharing girl stories."

Mam's eyes flashed to me, and I allowed myself a small shrug of discomfort.

***

Even with Aunt Bess around, I managed to fit in a few minutes a day with Soot. You'd think after the coney incident and then the eggs, I would have stopped working with the feathered beastie, but I was sure I could control her.

In hindsight, it was a mistake.

Soot watched from the fence post. She knew I had food. I waved a small piece of crispy pork rind in the air. Soot was suspicious, but interested. She glided closer, hopping agitatedly from foot to foot. I grabbed her and tethered her to the porch railing. She wasn't pleased, quorking so loudly the cat came out from the barn to investigate.

Da wiped his forehead of sweat. On the bottom step, Cam sat whittling on a three-hole pipe. Da paused to examine Cam's work, nodding approval. "Make a few more, and we can sell them at the fair with our hawks."

"Look, Da." I placed three half walnut shells before me. I wanted to show how clever she was. I hoped it would make Da smile. He was so sad lately. The worry lines on his face seemed permanently drawn.

Aunt Bess came to the window. I pretended I didn't see her.

Cam snickered. "A shell game for a raven?"

I smiled. "Think ye can guess better than Soot?"

Cam snorted. "Aye. I think I can."

Soot busied herself trying to remove the leg jess. I called her name, knowing I had to work fast before she got loose. With enough time, she could untie anything. She glared at me. I waved the meat before her. She went still. I could almost see her small brain working. Once she watched, I placed the pork rind under one shell.

"Ready?" I asked Cam.

"Aye."

"Here we go." I moved the shells round and round, slowly at first and then faster.

"So can ye guess?" I asked as I lifted my fingers away.

Cam pointed to the middle shell. I released the tether from the porch railing so Soot could move freely. She walked to the left-most nutshell and tossed it aside, gobbling up the rind.

Da whistled in admiration.

Cam wasn't a believer. "'Twas luck. She picked the first one she came to."

"Try it again?"

"Sure."

"Want to bet on it?"

He grinned at me. "Sis, I'm nae an eejit."

Will paused on his way to the water pump and gave me a wink.

Cam held Soot's tether while I fished another suet piece out. Soot's gaze followed my hand. I set it under the middle shell, sliding them around and around until *I* didn't know where it landed.

"So where?" I asked Cam.

"The left-most one. She's only choosing the first shell she comes tae."

Soot bobbed up and down with excitement. At my nod, Cam released Soot's tether. She hopped past the first two and flipped the last shell up. There was the rind. Soot swallowed it with a single toss. She then whistled, imitating Da.

Da watched, his eyes reflective. "Nell, she's clever, all right. But we both ken she's too clever."

How could she be too clever? Was there any such thing?

Chapter

25

Trying to keep up with the chores wore on me. I rose before dawn and laid my head down well past when the tawny owl high in our pines ceased its long halloos. And then only after making sure Will had settled. Some days, I could barely keep my eyes open past mid-afternoon.

Aunt Bess, her parasol protecting her head so the sun wouldn't bring out freckles, found me out back half asleep. She reprimanded me for avoiding her sewing lesson and tsked over my dusty clothes and mud-caked shoes. She didn't seem to understand that living on a croft wasn't a life that encouraged white gloves and a parasol. Getting a trained hawk to fly to a lure and return was no easy task. It didn't happen without hard, dirty work, long hours of cleaning cages, trapping prey for lures—none of it needing a lick of womanly art.

With all this on my plate, I wasn't in any mood to coddle her. How many days did I need to sew, anyway? It interfered with my real work—training raptors. I thought of Mam and gritted my teeth; only a little longer, and Aunt Bess would be gone. Our life would be back to normal, just Mam, Da, my brothers and, hopefully, the new babe. I dusted myself off, ignoring her patter that my freckles were showing, that my dress was dirty, even my breathing was too loud, and marched back to the house.

Da and Will barely glanced up from repairing the dray's wheel when I trudged past. As the door opened, Aunt Bess screeched. I dashed inside, worried about what had happened: Mam in labor or Ben cut himself with an axe again? Da and Will ran in behind me to see what was wrong.

Someone must have left the kitchen window ajar. Soot had taken it as an invitation and entered. She stood ankle deep in the last two pieces of berry pie. Ben was supposed to have put it in the pie safe, but he had run outside to fetch more water for Bess's morning wash. Soot never missed an opportunity to eat. Her bill was pink, her feet were pink, and the table was marked by pink raven tracks.

Aunt Bess grabbed the nearest thing, her parasol, and swung it across the table. Soot hopped away with me yelling, "Dinnae hurt her, dinnae hurt her," at the top of my lungs. With her next swipe, Bess barely missed clobbering my bird. Soot flapped to a high shelf with Bess chasing her, wailing away with that parasol. Two iron pots crashed down, and Da's pewter tankard landed with a bang. I raced around to help Soot, terrified at the vengeance in my aunt's eyes. Aunt Bess pursued Soot from the rough stone floor to the ceiling, bracing her parasol before her like a swordfighter as she cornered Soot up against the north wall. She looked bound and determined to end my bird's life.

Soot dove beneath the parasol and launched herself to the window before gliding off to a low branch on a nearby oak. From that relative safety, she screamed raven curses at my aunt.

Bess took a single step out the door before coming to an abrupt stop. She must have remembered her dainty, white, calf-high boots and the mucky, overgrown walk and reconsidered.

From the safety of her tree, Soot screeched, "Resist," over and over.

My Aunt never liked Soot, and the feeling was well returned, but this day it got taken to a full-blown war.

I looked for Da. I knew the bird would have to go now. There was no hope. I found him leaning over the fence, his face covered with a large handkerchief, his chest heaving.

It was worse than I thought. "Da, I'm sorry. Please dinnae make me kill her. I'll take her far away, I'll pick more berries, I'll…"

Da raised his head and choked out, "Yer bird's a disaster, Nell." I started to defend Soot again, but I realized Da was holding back a guffaw. "I'll miss that pie, but I haven't laughed this hard since before ye were taken." His shoulders shook with amusement. "The bird can stay, but try tae keep her away from Bess."

I nodded.

He cupped my chin, "And dinnae tell her I was laughing, lass. Let's keep it twixt ye and me."

For her part, Soot quorked and hissed from the safety of the barn windows whenever Aunt Bess deigned to step outside. I knew better than to rile a raven; they're birds with a long memory and a penchant for mischief.

***

The west field had been harrowed and manured. Da came in for tea and nodded, pleased with himself. "We are fortunate indeed. Nae everyone gets the luck we hae. Look at this, the sun is shining, the fields green. I hae a bonny wife, seven wonderful children, and one more babe on the way. How could anyone nae be happy?" Da clapped on his hat and walked back outside.

Bess had a smug expression on her face. She was still in a fluff from the day before. "Oh yes, the pastoral life of the crofter countryman." She looked pointedly around the room, taking in the worn furniture, the shawl knitted from wool remnants lying across the couch to cover the tears, the rocking chair nicked and scraped by the enthusiasm of six boys.

I got up and went outside, careful not to slam the door directly in Bess's face. Da was standing at the corral fence, pouring out the slop for the pigs. I walked over and lay my head on the fence post.

"What's with ye, lass?"

"She's hard to bear, Da."

Da flipped the bucket upright, his bad leg braced on the lowest fence rail. He knew who I spoke about.

"She's a sad woman, Nell." He sighed. "We both need tae give her some slack. She's a woman who never loved, never had bairns, never had purpose. A trinket tae sit on a shelf. Something bright to dust. Try tae walk in those fancy-heeled white shoes of hers and see how they pinch.

"Even before yer mam and I married, she was never a merry lass."

"But," I said, waving my hand toward the house, "look at her, she's rich, she's beautiful. What else does she need?"

"Aye, fine, obedient, dutiful, and chilly—a tiny prick of light on a match." He held up one finger and blew. "Unlike my Maura, who lights up any room she walks in like a warm, welcoming hearth fire on a winter's eve." He smiled to himself before continuing his story. "Bess always looked tae please, afraid of anything that her mother might nae approve. She was never a woman with much fire—then she had tae settle for George Thackery, yer mam's old suitor. After that, she nae seemed to smile; what little light she had was quenched.

"Yer grandmother did a right nasty trick, pushing them together after yer mam and I married."

My eyes must have widened as Da laughed. "Aye, I know what Bess says, but that's the truth of it. Yer mam and I eloped before her mother could post the bans for her and George." He looked over at me. "Dinnae get me wrong. George wasn't a bad man. He simply believed in his own irresistibility, and yer grandmother encouraged him. It was a hard fall fer him once he realized Maura eloped, married to another.

"I believe he did his best tae be a good husband to Bess, in the only way he knew. He gave Bess status and standing in their town, but little love."

"But she's rich."

Da patted my shoulder. "Aye, well, all that money 'tis in a trust, locked up in the land, and destined fer a far-off nephew of his."

At my startled look, Da shifted his weight. "Bess only gets a small allowance fer her clothes."

Da quieted, as if thinking back to that time. "Poor lass. Bess put up a good show fer her mother and fer herself." We both watched as the pigs dug into their dinner. "Pride is a rough steed tae ride, but Bess saddled it and has been riding that horse e'er since. But it must hae been hard knowing that she wasn't his first choice, truly nae his choice at all, just a way to save face. He'd been jilted."

Aunt Bess walked onto the back porch, beckoning at me to come inside. I pretended not to notice.

Da leaned over to me. "I dae believe that this is the happiest I've seen her."

At my incredulous look, Da nodded. "Ye won't get her tae admit it, but ye are giving her purpose, something that she has never had."

"Elizabeth Nellie," Aunt Bess called across the way, cupping her hands. She was only one hundred feet away. I could hear her easily from that distance. She didn't have to yell.

Da looked at me. "Sounds like she's wanting ye back inside."

"Dae ye think I can ignore her, just this once?"

Da grinned. "Dinnae we all wish. Go inside, lass. The fair is coming up soon, and we'll both escape her."

***

That night, hours after Roselyn's nightly pleading, I watched the lightning from the Tower off to the west. The blue and orange lights flashed, streaking across the darkened sky. I wondered if they'd cause another fire. And would I be blamed for it.

Will sat on a downed log, his shoulders taut. A whisper of words welled out of his lungs. "Soon. Soon, my love."

I joined him, leaning my head on his shoulder. Nothing more could I say that I hadn't said already, but I would not let him go and get snared. I'd go first.

Late that evening, Mam got worse. "A bit of blood, nothing much."

Aunt Bess got her to rest the following morning, and the morning after. It was the last time I saw my Da smile for many days.

Chapter

26

With Bess underfoot, the days dragged. She kept me at her beck and call from when she finally arose mid-morn to soon after supper, when she would retire to the couch, sitting poker-stiff like she was expecting a visit from royalty. Then she'd collapse to bed like she'd done a full day of work.

She emerged from my cubby-hole of a room like a butterfly from its chrysalis.

Cam clamped his mouth shut when she ran a finger over the kitchen counter and pointedly held it up. Tempers frayed wherever her frilly skirts swished.

How did she get this prissy? I looked down at the napkin laid across my lap. I didn't even recall putting it there. Is this where I was headed? It was no worse a twitch than picking one's nose. Of all the quirks I could have acquired from my Tower stay, this didn't seem so bad. I seemed stuck being a smidgeon tidier, and though Cam saw the napkin across my lap, he kept his trap shut.

He left without saying a word to her, slamming the door with a bang.

From my seat, I could see Mam in her bed. She gestured to me, a reminder to engage with my aunt.

With a sigh, I began. "Tell me about before. When ye and Mam were young. Was there anything ye liked to do?" Even to me, it sounded snotty. I drew a smile across my face, trying to undo my tone of voice.

She smiled at me, that haute look I had come to hate. "I used to love the dances your mother and I attended. I was younger, of course, and so not able to go about as much as she did. But I did have a little fling."

She held out her hand, displaying gold rings, but her smallest finger had a pewter band with curious encryptions.

My interest piqued. I rested my head on my arms as I leaned on the table.

"Sit up, Elizabeth." I slumped down even further. Our eyes clashed, and she decided not to push her luck. She went on with her story, shrugging like she didn't care. "There was a boy once. Someone I admired. Edwin was his name. We attended many of the same fetes, both of us shy. We gravitated together."

She bent toward me. "Mamma scolded me for spending so much time with Edwin."

I frowned, not understanding.

"Not making the social rounds as I should." She sighed. "It was so long ago."

"What happened to him?"

"His family sent him off to study." Bess bit her lower lip. "I was… disappointed… at the time. So sure he would come back for me." She shook her head. "It was just as well. Mamma would never have approved."

At the question in my eyes, she responded, "Though

his family was well-situated, it wouldn't have worked." She dropped her voice as she raised her hand again. "They were magicians." She wiggled her fingers, lifting her pinky. "I still have this from him. A small ring that he said had held magic." She shook herself. "Of course, it isn't worth a ha'penny. I keep it as a sweet memory."

I perked up and started to ask more, but Tim's screams made both of us jump. We finally calmed him down enough to figure out it was merely a large splinter in his foot—painful, but not life threatening. Aunt Bess put her fine needle skill to digging it out, and I used the opportunity to escape.

***

I woke that night, restless. I sat in my nightgown on the porch, still fretting over Dulce, thinking about Jonathan, worrying about Mam, worrying about my future. I kept thinking back to Jonathan and his grandmother, wondering if he would appear. Would he show up hating me, or would he understand why I hadn't told him? I chewed my thumbnail, leaving little jagged edges. There was no way he could forgive me. We could never be friends... or anything else.

So many things to stew about. Picking one thread from among the tangle seemed a chore in itself. Life seemed like one big, knotted worry.

Roslyn's voice wormed its way across the evening wind. Stepping off our porch, I avoided putting my feet into any dung deposited by our sheep. In the light of the full moon, my gaze pulled toward a puddle of water. The Guardian's face shimmed beneath the stars. "Child, listen to me! You're the only one I can call. Please, help me."

I kicked dirt across the water, watching the ripples break up his image. I wasn't a fool. My hands shook, and I grabbed them to stop the trembling. As my body stopped shaking, I noticed a lantern flickering in the barn. I padded over in my bare feet, wondering who was as restless as I was this night. Fidelus and Rowdy were nowhere around. Pepper raised his head but didn't consider me worth barking over, drifting immediately back into sleep.

Will turned as I entered the barn, the light in his eyes despondent.

"Hey, Sis." His haunted look lessened.

"Couldn't sleep either?" I asked.

"No, couldn't sleep. What are you doing up at this hour?"

"Just fretting. And ye?" I saw the bridle in his hands, his travel-worn leather pack leaning against the wall. The air turned around me with a twist as I realized what he planned.

"Ye were going to leave, weren't ye?" I said once I put it together. Roselyn's cries trailed across the night. I gritted my teeth. She couldn't leave him alone, not even for one night.

I heard a sigh, then saw him quiver as Roselyn called out again. The sorrow in his eyes hit me hard.

"Ye can't go. The Roselyn ye loved is gone! Ye need to accept it. Leave it be!"

"Sis, I still love her."

"It's over—done, Will." I thought back to the wraiths locked inside the Tower and the golden-haired magician who wove her web.

He shook his head, not believing me.

"Ye cannae imagine the lives she's ruined. If ye go to the tower, you'll be trapped like the others, locked inside those walls."

"She wouldn't do this. It isn't like her."

"I was there, remember? Held by her, I saw what she did."

He twisted the reins in his hands. "I could reach her."

"That's folly. Ye aren't a magician. That's what it would take, someone more powerful than her, even."

He seemed so wistful as he spoke. "Love is a kind of magic. Don't you think? Forgiveness and understanding. Magic is in the music we play and the feelings we share and in the sun rising each day."

I was tempted to shake him; he was such the dreamer. This wasn't an argument I could win, not at this hour of the night, anyway.

It was then I knew that Roselyn would never let him go. She'd never quit.

I had to go back to put an end to this, and soon.

"Dinnae go now. Please, for me, wait until after the fair, after Mam births. Please, Will." I heard another call, a whisper of her voice. Her pleading ached so much that even I was tempted.

We stood there for an eternity until he slowly nodded and replaced the bridle on its hook.

Together, we walked back into the house. Pepper didn't open his eyes but flapped his tail thrice as we walked by.

And I started my plans for returning—back to the Tower, but not with Will. Somehow, I had to break Roselyn's magic. I wondered about Bess's ring. Was it truly magic?

I didn't get much sleep.

***

I dragged myself out of bed the next morning. My eldest brother, Ned, came by to tell us a lightning strike took out a shed across town. He carefully avoided my eyes when he spoke.

Once I finished breakfast, I walked out to the pasture, mulling over this last fire, Roslyn's.

Will was out working his horses like nothing had happened. He spoke not a word about the night before. I didn't tell. But every time I looked his way, the need to return to the Tower burned inside me. Roselyn wasn't going to give up and the fires would not stop. How long would it be before someone was hurt or killed by one?

Each day, Roselyn's calls came. I shoved aside the wails that came at the end of each day when her voice would grab me about my guts.

I would look at Will. Watch his face alight when he heard her first call and then darken as though a candle were snuffed, before bending back to his work, his body stiff.

I scarcely slept that week, afraid Will would sneak past me in the night and be gone. But I couldn't chance returning until the babe was borne. The risks were too high.

Chapter

27

Aunt Bess was up early, at least by her standards. Outside the window, Soot was quorking and calling up a storm. I got dragged back to the house before I had finished my chores. Soot watched in indignation as I passed her by without offering a treat.

Cornered in our front room, Mam on one side and Aunt Bess on the other, they debated their next move. My hair braided into loops like it had been in the Tower. I'd finally conceded to some things, and this was one of them. It didn't get tangled up in things as much. The baths also made sense. Not that I had changed so much.

Even with that, Bess and I had a tussle over the ruffled pink dress she wanted me to wear. After a war of heated looks, Bess rummaged through her luggage and pulled out a simpler dress in lilac made of a silk so soft it felt like butter.

"I remember this gown. Mother had it made when I was sixteen," Mam said, running her fingers over the sleeve detail. It was the light in Mam's eyes that finally did me in. She looked so hopeful.

Bess nodded. "I found it when I was packing for here. Remember how the Templeton boys followed you around that night? They were sweet on you. Mother was so sure one of them would spark your interest."

I finally conceded to don it. Even I felt bonny as it slipped down my sides and fell lightly against my legs. Aunt Bess, after another comment on my stubbornness and ungrateful manners, knelt by my side, pins in her mouth, and began taking it up. A process I could only believe would be my undoing.

"Doesn't she look lovely?" Aunt Bess crooned.

The bones in the corset had me standing straighter than a fireplace poker. I had been tormented into a dress that, while I agreed was pretty, was only slightly better than an iron pen for comfort.

"Like a pig caught in a poke," Cam whispered as he walked by.

Tim started to climb on my lap, but Aunt Bess whisked him away, afraid a small boy's sticky hands might ruin her creation.

I looked at Da and Will, daring them to say anything. Both left quietly, with only a smile from Will and a flash of a wink from Da.

***

Two days later, a message arrived at midday tied with a ribbon, announcing the Simpsins' intention to come "sit."

Which meant they planned on looking me over.

This from a family whose second son, Derwin, I had trounced proper when he kicked our dog. 'Course, it was a long time ago; I was eleven and him pushing fourteen. As Mam says, people can change, and it was Angus who was seeking my hand.

Aunt Bess was all aflutter, clucking around our cottage like a hen who'd just laid an egg. Bollocks and double bollocks.

Bess was jubilant. "Everything must be scrubbed and cleaned

before the Simpsins arrive. Both elder boys, Angus and Derwin, are coming, and their mama. If they seem reasonable, we can encourage their attention. If not, others will see your worth. You know how word gets around." She acted like this was a good thing, and I was pretty certain it wasn't. She clapped her hands together. "The most important thing is to make a good impression, to let people know that you are a prize worth having."

Like a milk-fed heifer, I thought. But inside, I agreed with her—at least about the scrubbing. When had our house become so scruffy? I scoured the floor with vinegar.

Da frowned. "I told Maura I dinnae like those boys. They were nae so la-de-da before. Last I heard, this money is newly come by, and they're blowing through it faster than a lard-coated eel." But we both knew what he was thinking: that bull, a new black bull.

Bess turned to Da with a smug expression set on her face. "Jealousy is unbecoming. You're running down Elizabeth's first suitor before he's even arrived."

Dad snorted. "Oh, I ken them boys. You can smell their place a mile away. Money cannae fix what ails that clan. T'would be like gilding a toad."

Bess got the tiniest crease on her forehead, but then she shook her head. "I'll see for myself, thank you very much."

Mam looked from Da to Aunt Bess, but she didn't venture an opinion.

With everyone distracted, Soot took this as a welcome and hopped inside, snagging a single oatcake on Aunt Bess's plate. That might have been the end of it, but Soot had a liking for dust baths, and a pile of flour was more than she could resist. I could even understand Aunt Bess's initial scream when she saw the white-covered nightmare of a bird on our table, crumbling the remains of the oatcake. But the way Bess screeched, you would have thought we were invaded by bears.

Before I could react, Bess started after Soot again, grabbed her green and peach silk parasol, opening and closing it so fast it looked like some flying animal. The ribbons and bows flounced about like brightly colored bullfrogs upon a huge lily pad. For all that her reaction was overmuch, it took me a full hour to set the kitchen back to rights.

Da wasn't laughing this time. He hauled me out back, pointed to a cage, and said, "Lock her up."

By the next afternoon, when the Simpsins stopped by, our front room was presentable. The floor shone with bee's wax, and Bess had our garden flowers placed about in such a way that you didn't notice the dings in the furniture.

They came in a carriage so gussied up with bright colors it looked like a poppy. They hadn't properly prepped it. The paint was already peeling on the back fender.

Their mother's double chin fascinated me. It seemed to spring forth from below her ears like a pillow lying directly on her chest.

Her eldest son, Angus, was a big man with large hands and short, pudgy fingers. Not someone I felt an attraction to. The younger son wasn't much better, though he must have been three stone lighter. We also had our run-ins years before. Though I knew I should let that go.

Bess pulled her skirt away when he hawked up a big goober and spat. I could see her re-evaluating the wisdom of this meeting.

Mam acted like nothing was unusual. Da looked hard put to keep the I-told-you-so from his face, and I tried not to see them as thieves, 'cause maybe they weren't. They could have come by their bull honestly.

Aunt Bess tried to make the best of this, but I could see that she was appalled by their rough ways.

"We could use another hand around." Angus's mom looked over her missing neck, measuring my worth. "Sort of small, isn't she?" She looked at my hips like she could size up my ability to plow fields and birth babies at the same time. I felt like a banty

158

hen hemmed in by great hulking geese. Any minute, they would descend on me and peck.

For all Bess's self-control, she twitched when they sat near her. I could see her looking for lice. She wouldn't meet Da's eyes, avoiding his smirk like she had fallen into a big hole she should have avoided. She knew he had been right.

Bess put on a brave front; I'll give that to her. She distracted them with talk about her travels, offered them tea, talked about the weather. She did seem loathe to bring forth my handiwork with its crooked stitches, even to them.

Derwin kept looking around. "So, how much did you bring back?"

"What?"

"From the Tower. Coins, gold."

I looked at Mam before answering.

"None. There was none to bring back."

He looked at Bess's clothes and the rings on her fingers. He nodded and winked at me. I didn't wink back.

"But you've been in there."

"True." I answered, unsure where this was going.

"You could get back up there if you wanted." There was that annoying wink again. "Everyone knows."

"Knows what?"

"That you're just waiting to go get that gold."

I raised my voice. "There is nae gold."

Aunt Bess pressed one finger to her mouth. "Elizabeth."

How could I forget? Ladies never raise their voices.

Angus's eyes keep flickering out the window, but I couldn't see what grabbed his attention.

Mam, tucked into our rocking chair, tried to engage him in small talk. "I hear you've a fine new bull. He sounds like a good start for your herd."

He looked like she had speared him with a knife. It took even longer than usual for him to form a sentence. His mom cleared her throat and spoke for him. "Derwin won it in a bet."

Da cocked his head to the side, questioning. I agreed. Angus's mother and her boys all sat forward on their large bums as if waiting to flee. Da followed up with a question to Derwin. "What good fortune. What's the breed?"

A muscle in his cheek twitched. "Ah, don't know. He's big, though, well-muscled and strong. Gonna produce some nice calves."

Da turned and smiled, but I could see a glint in his eyes. "What color is it?" He leaned against the door, all casual-like.

Da knew what color. He had told us a month ago.

Angus jumped. "Black."

His eyes skittered away from Da's, landing at a single point on our braided rug. He swallowed. "Definitely black."

Da smiled again, but there was a look in his eyes that told a different tale. "Well, best o' luck tae ye." He pushed the door open and hesitated.

"If ye hear tell of a copper bull, I'd like tae know. Someone stole it from my lad two months past."

Derwin peered out the window again and, all of a sudden, stood, insisting it was time to leave. They shook themselves loose of the house, made their goodbyes, rolled into their carriage, and left.

Once they left the yard, I looked out the window, wondering what had caught his eye. There was only Will, working his horses.

Mam thanked Aunt Bess for arranging this visit, and they both agreed that Angus wasn't right for me.

But maybe, I thought, it was an answer about what had happened to Will.

Chapter 28

Soot leapt from the laundry post and fluttered out to the stump on a cut-down tree, making a ruckus about—nothing. Her screams of "thief" would wake up Mam. I grabbed her, held her beak closed, then narrowed my eyes, looking into the woods at the far end of our pasture. Nothing, again.

My brothers laughed when I confided someone was watching, mocking me about fearing my own shadow. Ben took to jumping out from dark corners and yelling, "Boo!" Cam sneered, calling me a nervous Nelly.

I didn't mention movements within tree shadows or the sounds of wheels beyond the pasture. It made it too easy for my brothers to tease me.

I busied myself with the kestrel. He hadn't been returning as well as I had hoped. I wanted to try another way to get his attention. So involved was I, it may have been the turning of an hour before I noticed the silence; no quorking, no screeches, no "resist," and no calls of "thief." Soot never went far from me, always seemed to keep me in her line of sight, like I was a shiny object for her to play with.

When I thought to hunt for her, it took me a long stretch, searching the tall grasses of the backfield, hunting around the barn. I couldn't believe she had left. There was no time to waste on a raven. I would be late for luncheon. My brothers would eat all the good stuff and leave little for me. But I couldn't bring myself to stop.

Pepper sniffed her out, nosing against the still, black body behind the henhouse. She was out cold. A large stone rested beside her. I almost cried when her eyes opened and she fluffed up with a shake.

Da sat the boys down, asking each in turn. "Fess up, lads. We ken that none of ye would hae tried to hurt Nell's critter, but maybe ye were just trying to scare it. If so, I would understand."

Cam spoke up, defending them all. "Da, none of us would dae such a thing. The raven is Nell's. She's hers tae deal with!"

No one confessed. But I wondered about my aunt. She hated Soot. After an afternoon, I gave that thought up. Bess couldn't throw worth nothing.

Within a day, Soot healed, but it set her back some, and she became even more insistent that something was watching. Someone in the woods. I believed her. Stones didn't fall out of the sky.

Chapter

29

I raced outside to get the wash off the line before the downpour. Thunderstorm clouds heavy with water roiled over toward me from the mountains in the east. Lightning flashed about two miles away.

Up the path coming fast, a rider hailed me. His cloak flapped in the strong wind, and his bay horse tossed its head. It was Jonathan. My body froze, and it was a half-second before I even breathed.

The clouds tumbled into one another, and a clap of thunder followed. Jonathan's horse trembled and stamped his feet.

"Get your horse in the barn," I called over the wind. As I pulled the wicker basket to the clothesline, the sheets flapped in my face. The wooden pins barely held them as they threatened to lift away. Behind me, the patter of rain plunked as the clouds moved across the pasture and hit the slate roof of the barn. The first stray drops were splattering across my face as Jonathan wrangled with the end of a sheet while I grabbed for Da's other shirt. The charcoal sky lit as lightning forked the sky and thunder shook the earth. Three socks tumbled to the ground before I could get to them. Jonathan hesitated over a boned corset of Aunt Bess's that danced before him. I reached over and unpinned the lacey bodice before he gathered his nerve to pluck it from the line.

The rain pummeled down as we grabbed the last of the things and made for the barn. Inside, Pepper dove under a haystack, shaking at each clap of thunder.

I was silent, not sure what to say now that he was here again. He put the wicker basket down near his saddle and went to calm his horse.

I couldn't meet his gaze, afraid of what I would see. The silence, broken by the crash of thunder and pelting of the rain, weighed on me.

"Jonathan?"

He pierced me with a look. "My grandmother spoke to me."

I hid my hands in the folds of my dress so he couldn't see them trembling. "I figured."

"So why didn't you tell me that Dulce is there and trapped?" He said it like I had betrayed him, and I had. "Am I so untrustworthy? Or did you not care enough to tell me?"

I blew air out my lips, all my excuses abandoning me. I started to stammer out an apology, but he stopped me with a glance.

Tears welled, and I scrubbed them away before they could spill. "Nae, that's nae it at all. Will was ill and hurt. I had to get him home first. I didnae know if ye would help me if ye knew about Dulce. The Tower's deadly. I dinnae know if anyone can be rescued from there."

Jonathan stared unblinking at me. "You could have talked to me."

Much to my dismay, my sniffling continued as tears overflowed. "I didnae want to give ye false hope." Worse, once I started talking, I couldn't seem to shut my mouth. Words kept pouring out. "I was so afraid of going back." My voice dropped to a whisper as I confessed. "Afraid of getting caught again and afraid of Will dying."

He sat down on a milking stool and heaved a sigh.

I was scared to look at him again. Scared of what I would see in his eyes.

"I might have done the same."

I peered down at him, checking to see if he was placating me. "Truly?"

"Yes, truly."

We sat listening to the rain pounding on the roof. I fidgeted.

"You're hiding something, aren't you?" he asked.

I met his gaze.

He guessed it. "You're considering going back."

I nodded. "I've seen the Guardian many times since I left. He's spoken to me."

"Where? How?"

"In the water of the goat trough, in the puddles of rainwater, in a bucket of wash water, anything that reflects light. He says the Tower is failing, along with everyone there: Roselyn, the wraiths, and him."

"Do you think he's lying? That it's a trap?"

"Maybe, likely. But I have to try—for Dulce and for Will. I'm the only one who has escaped."

"You're willing to risk your life? For my sister?"

"Yes, for her and for my brother... and for ye," I admitted. "Dulce helped me. She encouraged me to nae give up." My mouth spoke before I could stop myself. "And you're a friend to me."

He seemed to consider this. I did, too—a friend. My face

flamed. Maybe he didn't feel the same way. Maybe he only saw me as a way to get into the Tower, a tool, a servant.

He finally nodded. "When?"

I suppressed a sigh of relief that he didn't call me on it. "My mam's soon to birth, and the last baby…"—I dropped my voice—"didn't make it."

He nodded again, understanding.

"Da needs this fair. We need the coin it will bring. Once 'tis behind us and Mam's babe is born, I'll go, just once, and see if I can help those trapped. And to destroy it if I can't."

"I'm going with you."

My head snapped up. "I don't need anyone's protection."

"Maybe—but you have it. We're friends, remember?"

I blushed again, hoping he couldn't see.

He leaned closer, his shoulder almost touching mine. His voice lowered. "Do you think there is any hope for my sister?"

Under the thunder, I could hear Aunt Bess calling. She didn't seem able to let me alone for a moment. I ignored her. Let her wait. This is more important than fussing with dresses and the proper way to serve tea.

Was there any hope? Maybe. I didn't know for sure. Maybe Bess's ring was magic and would be enough, or maybe it was just a plain old pewter ring.

"One thing I did learn from that month in the Tower is there is always room to hope. It costs naught."

He looked at me long, then.

"And what do you hope for, Nell?" He was so near, it was hard to get my words together.

I shrugged it off. "Right now, I hope for coin to pay our bills and that Will gets free from Roselyn."

The rain was slacking off when Bess toodled over with her silly sun parasol, the same one as before: silk, green, and peach, and, as she had let us all know, had come straight from London.

"Elizabeth, who is this?" She looked at us sitting together. "You shouldn't be here without a chaperone to oversee you."

I bristled. "It's Jonathan, Aunt Bess, the one who helped me bring Will back."

"Oh, yes. Jonathan." She eyed him like a prospective suitor. "We weren't expecting a caller. Please step inside. I'll put on a pot of tea so you can visit with Elizabeth."

"'Tisn't like that," I said, unable to look Jonathan's way.

She patted my hand like I was a small child needing instruction. "Jonathan, you must excuse Nell. She's naïve in the ways of the world. We don't want anyone to get the impression that you're taking advantage of our girl, now, do we?"

I didn't stay to hear what happened after. I stormed off, embarrassed by her talk and misunderstanding. I daren't hope that Jonathan was interested in me in that way. I knew he had a lass. We had a common bond, nothing more than that. Both of us had kin magicked by the Tower.

***

That night, I sat with Mam. She looked so pale and wan that I hated to bother her, but she was my only hope of reining Aunt Bess in. "Mam, make her stop."

"What happened, Nell?"

"She embarrassed me in front of Jonathan."

"Bess mentioned that Jonathan and you were out in the barn."

I blurted out all at once, "She made a fire out of two sticks of wood. Nothing was happening. He came about his sister, not as a suitor."

Mam planted a kiss on my forehead. "This is hard, isn't it, sweetheart, changing from girl to woman? The rules are not to your liking."

Bollocks. Mam would side with Aunt Bess. "You should

have heard her, Mam. It was horrible."

"She was wrong to embarrass you that way, but she is right. You're of the age when people judge you, and judge harshly if you are alone with a man."

I tried again. "But it was Jonathan."

"And you're a lovely, comely lass."

I sulked. "I just want to go back to the way I was."

"You can't stop, love. It's past that."

Chapter

30

After that, I tried, really, to return to who I had been, refusing to do anything Bess suggested, fighting her like a rooster headed for the chopping block. I blamed her for my troubles and set myself against any that smacked of her fancy life. I didn't wash that next morning. I let my hair hang down and put on my oldest patched dress, even though it was too tight around the chest.

Surely, she would give up after a few days of my proving I was a lost cause.

I had just played a series of jigs on my fiddle before I went outside, whistling, working through a harmony I wanted to add.

Bess stood at the door, her green and peach parasol in hand in case the sun dared to shine on her skin. "A whistling girl and a crowing hen never come to any good end."

I was tired of her. Nothing we did was right: my da was

common; my brothers were too rough, too loud, and too many. Mam's breeding problem caused by her marrying beneath her.

"Are you a shining example of a non-whistling girl?" I snapped. Aunt Bess's face closed up, and she disappeared into the house.

I felt bad, but not that bad. We both kept our distance the rest of the day. I didn't know where she was, and I didn't care. My hawks needed training. I turned my back on her and all that she meant.

***

Even though Bess and I were at cross-points, Mam pressed me to see one more suitor. She looked so peaked that I couldn't refuse, though, given my first suitor, I hadn't much faith there would be any improvement.

Bess perked right up when the Bledsoes came. Respectable, middling money, and from a family only one village away, or at least that's what Bess kept prattling before they arrived. Once they arrived, it became clear I wasn't the ideal choice for their mother.

Aunt Bess welcomed Molly Bledsoe and Bill, her silent but annoying son. Mam sat quietly on our only stuffed chair. Molly eyed each item as though calculating the price of everything in our living room and thought it come up wanting. I wished she would stop her nodding and wipe that overly smug smile off her face. Her son, Bill, watched me like a sweet he might grab and devour.

Da noticed. Mam chivied him out of the house, as he was getting a mite protective.

"Well, dear, what do you do in the evenings after helping your Ma? Baking?

"Nae."

"Sewing?"

"Nae."

"No?"

"Aye, nae."

"Weaving?"

I put her out of her misery then, as she was working hard to understand. "I work hawks."

After a suitable silence, where she made it clear that I must have misunderstood, she asked, "No, what kind of sewing do you do?"

"I braid jesses." From the look on her face, she wasn't impressed.

Bill asked me to show him my hawks. I thought he might actually be interested, but it wasn't so. He kept sliding his arm around like to corral me. I sidled out of his reach most times. But once he put his sweaty hand around my shoulder. I yanked away with little grace. At least I didn't slap it.

Later, as they pulled away from our yard, Mam circled her arm about my waist. "I'm not sure if this would be ideal for you. Perhaps we should tell Bess to discourage their interest."

Cam felt the need to add his tuppence in. "It might help to get ye married off if ye would smile and dinnae look like ye swallowed a toad."

He shut up after I swatted him.

Now Aunt Bess and I had more to fight about. She blamed me for the caliber of my suitors, and I blamed her for trying to make me into a prissy girl. Da, though thoughtful, could not hide his glee that those suitors were vanquished. He, like me, didn't care why they were gone. Although Mam tried to be positive, I could see she was disappointed.

If that wasn't enough to mess up my week, there was Soot's newest scrape to deal with. Not that I wasn't sympathetic to her.

It had started, of course, when Bess had chased Soot with

her parasol, twice. Soot wasn't one to forgive or forget. And payment was due, at least in the mind of a raven.

At Bess's scream, Da and I charged over, looking for the fire. There was nothing out of place but the remains of a silk peach parasol. It was outside, dragged into the pig pen, bows and ribbons shredded.

Bess must have been more than fair-dancing-mad as she braved the muddy path into the hog hollow and grabbed her parasol between two gloved fingers. I cringed as it dripped pig manure across her leather-palmed hand. Immediately, she did a dance worthy of any Highland Scot, waving her hands and shaking them, all the time sinking deeper and deeper into the mud. Soot watched from the safety of our weathervane, bobbing up and down in raven glee.

While Da didn't approve and sure didn't want a raven this destructive, it took him some effort not to laugh. He grasped the door and excused himself, disappearing into the barn, howling in great honking gasps. I was happy to see Da laugh again.

I laughed too, but Bess saw me. She turned her back to me—so I spent more of my time with the hawks.

***

Though Bess remained with us, she wasn't quite as puffed-up as she had been. She refused to let go of her upset. Her eyes drifted to her damaged parasol leaning outside the back door, placed so we would all be reminded of her loss: her favorite silk parasol.

She glided about our home, as out of place as a swan in a duck puddle. We all knew she didn't fit in, and now she recognized it as well. Though I wanted her gone and relished her comedown, I didn't wish her harm. She was my aunt. Her being here kept Mam company, forcing her to sit for a part of the day.

Soot hissed at Bess but left it at that. I pointedly ignored her. She'd be leaving as soon as Ma birthed, which was only another handful of weeks. Surely, I could last that long without insulting my aunt again.

***

Our evening meal was somber as Mam took to bed with exhaustion. After dinner, the boys dispersed to their chores. Bess wandered outside to view the stars, and I cleaned up. I couldn't help but see Da walk in. In the dark of the bedroom, he sat next to Mam, his hands wrapped around one of hers. There are some scenes you don't want to know about. Things that are private. But this one caught me unawares. By the time I figured out what they were going on about, I was too caught up to leave.

"I will nae lose ye, Maura. Nae like this. Nae fer the lack of money." He pressed her hands to his mouth. "Why did ye ever marry me?"

"It is so obvious to me why I married you."

Da murmured something that I missed as I turned my head to see a shadow appear at the side door. Bess had returned.

Da said, "Ye certain ye want Bess tae stay?"

"She's a comfort to me, Nat. I love my sister. I know she puts on airs, but it's all she has."

Da sighed. "She's never lifted a finger in her life. How is she helping?"

Mam's soft voice responded, "Her presence helps; it's another woman in the house. You've got to give her credit for coming. She is used to luxury and servants, neither of which is a remote possibility here."

Da sagged. "Would that I could give ye diamonds and silks, my love."

She placed her hand over his mouth. "Nat, do you really believe that's what I want? I'm happy that she has luxuries to comfort her on a cold winter night. I have everything I need. More than I dreamed possible. I couldn't wish for more."

"I feel fer her. Truly, Maura, I do. Ye and I hae everything. And she's a forty-six-year-auld woman, widowed o'er twenty-five years. Nae children, nae husband. Nae one tae love or be loved by. 'Tis very sad."

I saw Bess creep out the side door, and I followed her. She had to have heard. She stopped at the side of the barn, leaned against the rough, gray siding, and sobbed. I left, unsure of what to say. But I bided my tongue after that and tried not to hurt her feelings again.

Chapter

31

I felt Jonathan's presence as I worked the hawks in the back pasture. He leaned quietly against the big ash that provided the only shade in our lower meadow. A few lengths away, Chloe watered their horses. She gave me a shy smile and raised a hand in greeting. I smiled back, careful-like, unsure of her real feelings.

I tried to give off a casual yet friendly air, but my heart beat so hard I was afraid he might hear it thumping. Soot called out, 'Resist' and followed up with a low wolf whistle. She wasn't helping.

"So..." He waved his arms about. "Is this out in the open enough for your aunt?"

I gave my best indifferent shrug. "She's napping. Da's over by yon burn, trimming lamb's feet, so nae one can say 'tisn't proper."

"I can't stay long. We promised Grandmama we'd join her for tea." He pointed down the narrow curve of the town road as her carriage pulled up to the edge of our property.

Her coachman helloed to Pa.

Da gently placed a flailing lamb next to its dam and, crook in hand, limped through the purple thistles and yellow gorse to pay his respects. The carriage door opened, and he bent forward, listening.

"Is everything right with her?" I asked, wondering why she stopped to talk to my Da.

"Yes. She's…" He looked up at the sky, as if the answer might come from above. "It's…"

I frowned but checked the sky also. It was a fine, bonny day.

"About the Tower," he finally said. "What else might we need to get into the Tower?"

"Ladder, gloves, rope." I tried to think what else would help. I clicked my tongue. "Magic, that's what your grandmother said. That's what we don't have." I hedged, only hedged, about the ring. It was only a simple pewter band, after all. Probably not magic, even if I could get it from my aunt.

I warned him again. "This may be a losing proposition." I didn't say that I planned on being there and back before he or anyone else noticed. I couldn't bear him harmed.

He rubbed his hand across his forehead, wiping the sheen of sweat off.

"That's nae why you're here. Is something wrong?"

"Ah." He hesitated. "There's trouble brewing. Folks think that the bad things happening are caused by the Tower."

"Likely," I acknowledged.

He sat on the porch railing as if contemplating his next words. "They're thinking you're the cause of it."

"What? I… I… nae," I finally got out.

"Worse, boys are lining up, daring each other to go to the Tower, wanting to prove themselves. Now that you're back, people think it is safe."

A chill slid down my back. "Still? Why?"

"Gold. They still believe there is gold."

I sputtered, "I've told everyone who might listen. There is naught there. Why dinnae they believe me?"

"People only believe what they want. There's one more thing." He looked deep into my eyes, and some part of me purred like a petted cat. "Some think you are the key to get the gold."

That doused my imagination forthright. My face must have registered my shock, and I couldn't speak. Jonathan's grandmama's carriage rattled off in the distance, and Chloe signaled they had to get going.

"Nell, be careful!" He stepped closer.

My heart betrayed me by doing flip-flops.

"Woo-hoo," Aunt Bess called from our porch, waving a flowered handkerchief. Bollocks, she was up.

Chloe and Jonathan swung up on their horses and trotted off. Tears welled, and I berated myself for being misty-eyed at his leaving.

I ignored my aunt and swung over to join Da, chewing on a hay stalk. He stared at the disappearing carriage. As I approached, he looked at me for a long time until I worried what he saw in my face.

His hand scratched at the stubble on his chin. "Tell me, lass, dae ye fancy that lad?"

"Da, nae ye too?"

He said nothing.

I ducked my head. "Da, please. I cannae bear to be teased anymore. Ye said it yourself; they're city folk and way beyond my ken."

He lifted my chin, which had dipped to my chest. "Lass, nae one is above ye. Yer worthy of a prince tae me. Worth more than gold or any coin."

I wrapped my arms around about him and sniffled into his rough shirt.

Da tucked his head on mine. "I'll nae speak a word to Bess or yer mam. But just between us, the two of us, dae ye have a liking fer him?"

I nodded into his shirt. "Aye."

He took in a huge breath then. I couldn't tell if he was disappointed or just sad for me.

Chapter

32

Bess remained subdued after hearing Da and Mam speak, like a butterfly wilting in the heat. I tried to be nicer to her, as she looked so sad.

She perked right up when Jonathan stopped by, before wilting again when he left without staying for tea.

I had been uncomfortable when he last came—I could barely meet his eyes. I couldn't tell Bess he only came because he hoped to rescue his sister, Dulce. Not only wouldn't she believe me, she'd try to stop me, and I needed her ring.

Da was as good as his word and didn't mention Jonathan by word or deed. My feelings about that lad were a tad raw.

In a rare instance of good that came from our problems, I didn't have time to be all moody.

With all the fuss and trouble besetting my kin, I made doubly sure to keep my eyes on Will. I watched as he worked, watched him turn his back to the west away from the Tower. Watched the muscles bunch in his back with the effort. Roselyn wasn't much heard that week. It seemed to me she quieted. If I listened carefully when I saw Will stop and stare, I could barely hear her keening. Mostly, her voice merged with the wind and the rain and the frogs croaking. It gave me hope that soon Will wouldn't hear her either. Still a voice in my head wondered: Was she giving up? And if she did, would she, Dulce, and the Guardian die or linger on in that half-life forever?

I had just mucked out the sheep pen when Mam asked for a song. Da was eager to oblige. He picked up his fiddle and started tuning, the signal for the rest of us to get out our instruments. I straightaway washed my hands out at the pump, smiling as Ben scooted by carrying freshly picked plums in a withe basket.

Cam called out, "Leave 'em on the porch. I'll get them after."

Ben set them down, latching the lid before racing for his violin. Bess pretended not to be interested, but she kept giving Mam's harp surreptitious looks. We all sat round the front room, squeezing Bess into the kitchen, her foot tapping time. Mam stayed in her bed, knitting a blanket for the new babe, positive that all would be well.

Da turned to her after the first song. "What would ye like tae hear, luv?"

"Something bright and cheery. Something that speaks of spring and flowers."

Da looked at Bess and then Mam's unused harp pushed into the corner.

"Bess, why dinnae ye play? Maura's harp is tuned."

She laughed a tinkling, brittle laugh. "Country music, I don't know them." But her fingers twitched.

Da insisted. "Come on, Bess. 'Twill please Maura tae hear ye strum a bit. Ge it a try. Think 'twill taint yer concert training?" He threw her a challenge. "I've nae been much for gambling, but I'd lay money down that ye can keep up with the best of us."

She tilted her head like she was searching for a retort. Her pride must have warred with her snooty dislike of our music, or maybe she was just bored. She wiped her hands clean on a dishrag and then settled down before Mam's harp. Da nodded to her and counted down a beat to start.

We had a good session. Ten songs played. I couldn't help but notice that Aunt Bess was a superb player, someone the trees would bend to hear.

Tim went back to the front porch, and I heard him exclaim. We all gathered at the door, pushing to see what was wrong. Bits of pecked black and red plums were scattered across the floor. The table was colored with red. And there was Soot, sitting on the basket, looking very pleased and stuffed. The cord holding the basket closed had been neatly untied.

No one spoke to me that day. I took Soot five miles out, climbed a tall pine and planted her on a branch. I cried all the way home.

The next morning, she was back, sitting outside and quorking for attention.

Da's eyes turned to me, and I burst into tears.

Da shrugged. "Try tae keep yer wee beastie from causing more harm."

Chapter

33

Half a week later, Soot quorked out an alarm. I'd taken to ignoring her warnings. I'd tired of looking over my shoulder—nothing was ever there but the regular flashes of light from the Tower. But as long as Will stayed home, I didn't care. The sun was setting, and I was busy putting my hawks away, shoveling out the mules, and locking up the rookery. Pepper lifted his head on the chance there was a deer to chase or pigs rooting around the scrub. There must have been, as he bounded to his feet and scurried off to the tree edge, barking loudly.

Bess came to the back door, holding her hands to her ears, pretending that the noise was too much for her to bear. I trotted off, yelling at Pepper to shut his yap, but he was beyond listening. He disappeared into the woods, baying like he was a fierce guard dog instead of a gentle old sheepdog. I heard a yelp, and the barking stopped.

I broke into a run. Soot whooshed along behind me, gliding

low to the ground, landing with a hop on a low pine stump. She arched her wings, letting out a series of harsh hisses.

Pepper lay on the ground, a large stick nearby, his eyes big with shock. I should have been suspicious then, but I wasn't. I was running on two candle-breaths of sleep. I didn't even see the two hooded men until they jumped out from behind the trees. They grabbed for my arms as I fought, screaming at the top of lungs. An elbow caught me in the jaw. My head flew backwards, but I must have gotten in a good solid kick, as I heard him grunt. The other thug took a hold about my waist and carted me off. I was losing badly. A bite to his hand seemed to discourage him until his buddy twisted my arm behind me. I screamed again, this time in pain.

This wasn't good. They were big men. I couldn't fight both. There was a flutter of wings, and one of them hollered. Blood oozed from three gashes under his torn shirt. The other continued dragging me. I heard him grunt once more, and I dropped to the ground. When I looked again, the two cloaked forms disappeared into the cover of the trees.

Aunt Bess stood with her remaining parasol outstretched, dirt upon her face. "Are you harmed?"

"No." Aside from a nasty bruise that was likely to bloom on my jaw, I wasn't much worse for wear.

Bess bent over suddenly, holding her diaphragm as she struggled for breath.

"My corset is not meant for running," she gasped out. I looked at her shoes. The once pristine, white-laced shoes were brown with dirt, her dress askew. Somewhere along the way, her bonnet must have flown off.

"Are ye harmed?" I asked her.

She shook her head, a funny smile on her face. "I haven't run that fast since I was twelve and Johnny Methone chased me with a frog." She looked me over again. "And you're truly not harmed?" she asked.

I raised up on one elbow, moving cautiously, as everything seemed to hurt. No bones broken, no open wounds.

"I'm sore, but naught that cannae be healed."

"You gave me quite a fright." She plopped down beside me, taking in two more deep gulps of air. "Here I thought country life was too quiet and wished for some excitement. I won't make that mistake again."

"Hmph." I rolled over to Pepper's side and ran my fingers over his legs. He was in shock and panting. Nothing broken that I could feel. There was a large lump on the side of his head and a bruised and mashed leg. They must have bashed him with the stick.

Soot sat on a low branch repeating "thief," over and over. In her talons was a piece of bloodied green cloth.

Will and Da hailed me from across the field. I tried to stand, but my head spun such that I couldn't and had to lean up against a sturdy sapling. Da took Aunt Bess's arm as Will carried me to the house.

Pepper was allowed to stay inside for a few days. He limped around the house, holding up his paw to anyone walking by. Da and the boys scoured the forest, looking for tracks.

Aunt Bess made peace with Soot, praising the bird for coming to my rescue. She shared her dinner with Soot that evening, picking out choice morsels of meat for her, even allowing her to sit on the windowsill overlooking our meal. Soot appeared to re-evaluate Bess. My Aunt elevated from villain to provider, somewhat like a wolf, a beast to be wary of, but one that could be useful.

The torn green cloth I put beside me that night, tucked into a small pouch in case I ever saw a shirt missing a swatch of that green.

My brothers debated. Where were those villains from? Why would anyone want to nab our Nell? Will said little, but his eyes were sick with worry. This had to be about the Tower, but none of us were willing to admit that—each keeping mum for our own reasons.

The only good that came from this was that Mam no longer put me out for show. Someone was after me and Mam wanted me close.

***

Da grew quieter. He rose up earlier than ever, searching the woods, scouting the land, fretting about Mam. I caught him at our money jar, all tipped out on the worn kitchen counter, counting our coin. Almost nothing there. It hurt my heart to see Da so despondent. The grief in his eyes was more than I could bear.

Mam rested her hand against the bedroom door, as if we couldn't tell she was using it to hold herself up. "We don't need money, Nat. I have you. We'll get by, like we always have."

"Did ye sleep at all?"

"It is no matter. I'm getting plenty of rest."

Da hastened to her side, his hand around her waist, easing her out the front door and into the wicker chair on the porch.

"This will turn around. I'll be up and about as soon as the babe is borne."

Da tucked a blanket around her swollen ankles and sat next to her until she fell asleep.

Later, I heard a lone fiddle, someone playing the saddest song. I wandered out to see. There was Da, his head hung down, his shoulders slumped like all the joy was beaten out of him, playing a tune that would break the heart of any who heard.

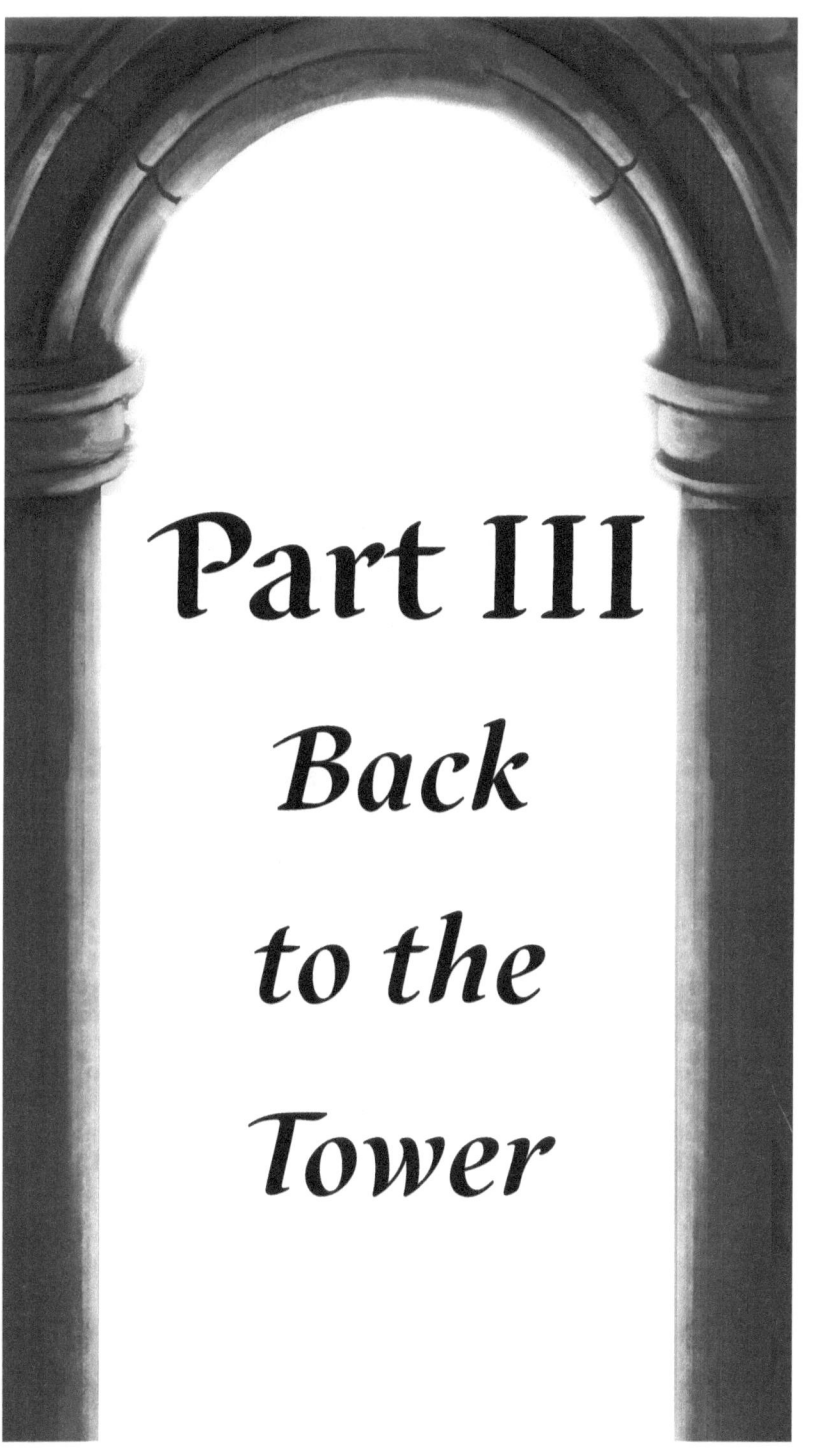

Part III

Back

to the

Tower

Chapter

34

Three days passed, and there wasn't time to fret about this or to wonder about the men who tried to grab me, though Will or Ned made sure to keep me in view. I set myself to the tasks ahead.

I had to finish my birds, readying them for the fair. And after? My climbing gear was assembled. I just needed to think of some reason to borrow Aunt Bess's ring and hold on to it for a bit. I'd return it once the Tower problem was solved. If I survived, that is.

I knew Jonathan thought we were going together, but I planned to stop Roselyn by myself. I would be there and back before anyone knew of my going. Last thing I needed was Will or Jonathan involved in this. No need to put anyone else in danger.

The afternoon before we headed to the fairgrounds, Da and I gathered all our birds and supplies onto our dray. Mam's time neared—less than two weeks. While she was up some each day, more and more she sat in her rocking chair, knitting or mending clothes. She wearied easily. Da had a permanent crease between his eyes.

The night before we left, I tossed and turned, excited about the fair, wondering if Jonathan might be there, hoping my birds would sell, and hoping for Mam's health.

Da fretted over leaving her, but Bess almost pushed him up the roadway. Mam stayed her usual down-to-earth self. "'Tisn't far; less than a half-day's walk, fifteen miles, nae more."

Mam gave me a kiss and some last-minute advice. "Remember what you promised. Look around you while you are there. Maybe some special someone will catch your eye."

Da glanced at me. He opened his mouth like he was about to speak and then reconsidered. I frowned.

Then Da reminded Hal and Ned repeatedly to stay near the house in case the villains came back around.

Will sat on the porch, cleaning his saddle. "Mam's safe. It was Nell they were after. They want the gold from the Tower, and they think Nell can get it for them."

I repeated, as I had so many times before, "There is nae gold there. I crawled every inch of that stone monstrosity."

Will stared at me, his eyes flat. "I know, but no one outside of this house believes you." He stared off to the west again before rubbing more oil into the cantle.

Da frowned at the two of us before addressing Mam. "Maura, you're nae tae exert yerself. Absolutely nothing, nae even tae pick up a handkerchief off the floor. Hal's staying close, and he'll dae all the heavy work.

"And Bess, keep yer parasol nearby. Ye sure pack a wallop with it."

Bess laughed. "We'll be fine, Nat. It's you who need to be cautious. You and Nell."

Will pulled me aside. "Nell, stay within hollering distance of Da or me. Things are badly amiss."

I shrugged and walked outside, not pleased with the kind of

attention I was getting. I was no baby. I could handle myself.

Once we returned, I'd ask Bess for the ring, and then I'd go back to the Tower.

***

My head kept turning as I searched the grass-covered road for Will. He had one last load of wood to deliver to our east-side neighbors before he could join us, only a few hours' work. Once I saw him coming up the road behind us, I realized how much I had been fretting.

Five sturdy cages held our hawks, bouncing at every dip in the dirt road. Soot came too, not that she was invited. She had followed. Nothing I did had seemed to discourage her, sometimes riding atop the cart, sometimes flying overhead, landing on the occasional fence post as her wings still were not strong enough to fly a long way. She was smart enough to keep her distance from Da.

Da walked across the fairgrounds, pushing the dray before him. I trotted after with my favorite peregrine on my arm. He led us up and down the aisles, looking at all the booths set up. "Nell, this is our fair. I ken it."

He sounded more like himself than he had in weeks. Will seemed gray and distracted. I nattered at him as we wandered about. We stopped before a fenced brace of spotted pigs before rounding the corner. At the edge of my vision, I spied Angus and Derwin hauling on a big black bull before they disappeared into the crowd, and I knew.

Da turned my way and pointed to a spot to set up our stall between a candlemaker and a hatmaker. "This is a fine location, far enough away from the farrier and the dyer so the noise and smell dinnae frighten our birds." He plunked down his hat and started unloading. "This year, we're going to win the grand prize for our hawks. They are prime. Ye've trained them well. But we need something better to attract customers. Some gimmick to keep the attention of the crowd." The way he spoke, it almost sounded like a prayer. Will barely glanced up from busying himself with setting up our booth.

Once our birds were safely settled, Da rocked back on his heels, admiring our work. "Looks good, my bonny bairns. What say we take a turn around the fair before the crowds arrive?" Before we left, the fair manager offered Da a deal. A cheaper booth price if he played a few rounds of tunes for the dancers. Ian, the candlemaker, offered to watch our booth. Da couldn't hide his delight. He grabbed his oak fiddle and handed an ash one to Will. My favorite of maple and spruce he handed to me, but I had bigger things in mind. Far and away, I had heard a bull bellowing over the brass horns, lowing cows, belled dancers, and other fair racket. I needed to shake loose of Da and Will. That bull had to be Will's.

We'd only begun our circuit when, in the distance, we saw Jonathan coming our way. My throat tightened and my chest palpitated.

He had a ready grin and carried a bag overflowing with peppermints. I could smell them from here.

Once he joined us, he turned to Da. "Might I keep your daughter company?"

Da narrowed his eyes and stared at Jonathan, searching. Finally, he gave a sigh and, with a slow half smile, said, "Aye. Be careful with my lass; she's a treasure."

Da was taking this too seriously. It was only a turn of phrase.

After Da and Will left, Jonathan and I walked a few paces, then he turned to me. "So Nell, do *you* mind?"

I stuttered a step. There it was again, implied courting. Every time we were together, he said something. "Ah…"

He offered me a peppermint. "Or perhaps you wish the time alone. I could understand entirely."

Was he truly interested in courting me? I wasn't sure I believed that, but would I mind if he kept me company? I knew I wouldn't mind at all.

I nodded, suddenly shy. "I'd love your company."

As we walked along, I was suddenly as tongue-tied as a netted fish. All I could think of was Mabel and what Arnold had told me.

When I could no longer stand it, I bumbled out, "What happened with ye and your Lady?"

His head spun toward me. "What?"

"Mabel. Arnold said ye were offering for her."

He turned three shades of red. "Brother or no, Arnold is a jackass. Mabel is a cow! A very good cow, it's true. And, yes, I've made a deal to buy her. There is no other girl."

Our eyes met and caught. Mine fell first as I tried to hide my chagrin. He must take me for a fool. But inside, my heart leapt.

Jonathan held out his hand. "How about a dance and we talk more later?" And he dropped the subject.

We only had time for two dances. Da's fiddling had everyone in a bonny mood. I felt his eyes on us as we twirled and bowed through the dance. Even Soot, watching the dancers from a high pole, bobbed to the music. Jonathan and I parted soon after. But as I fussed with my birds, my mind kept returning to Jonathan's words. Might I keep your daughter company?

Even if he didn't have a promised lass, it just wasn't possible.

I would never be a city Lady, and Jonathan, with his high-stepping horse, white linen shirt, and tailored trousers, was no crofter. There was no world where Jonathan and I could possibly be courting. And I called my brother a dreamer! Ha!

But he didn't have a lass—he never had. My thoughts scurried back through all our conversations. My heart pounded. It was a good thing my feet knew where the ground was, as my thoughts floated among the clouds.

It was only later that I realized I forgot to check on the bull.

***

Da's voice carried halfway across the glen as he worked the crowd. Standing like this, I could see why Mam married him. He was a looker. Even with his mustache now speckled with gray, he struck a fine picture. Head thrown back as he called out to passersby, "Merlins, peregrines, kestrels, trained and ready tae hunt."

Will, after tethering each bird on their perch, disappeared into the crowd. I stood at Da's left, checking my birds' feathers for any sign of lice. Da pointed over at me as my peregrine stepped onto my gauntlet.

"Look at my lass. Even a delicate thing like her can handle a big strapping bird."

Some highborn gentry, a man and his lady wife, hesitated. I tried to look delicate.

"Think what yer Lady can dae with a fully trained and gentled bird. It will perch on her arm as she rides out tae the hunt, the picture of Edinburgh fashion and elegance." Couples walked on by, stopping only long enough to nod and smile at Da.

My raven glided into view, eyeing the situation. She would ruin Da's show. I shooed her away, but she was hell-bent on joining me. She knew I kept food in my pouch when working hawks. Da noticed too and added her into his patter. "My friends, here's a treat, something ye willnae see anywhere else at this fair, nae in our whole county. See there? A raven, wild as the mountains themselves. My Nell can even call down these black fiends from the forest, the followers of wolves, the dealers of death."

I snorted.

Da kept up his spiel. "For ordinary folk, 'twould be a task beyond imagining, but my little lass manages these tricksters with her pure and gentle ways, the same way as she trains our hawks. They dote on her sweetness and charm, eating out of her hand."

Da was stretching to make this sound important, making me sound important. Da had never named me sweet and charming before. Stubborn and headstrong, sure, and I was great with birds;

none other could match my ability to calm a wild one. But Soot was only a common raven. Her craw drove her, not some great love of me. Or at least mostly, I thought, recollecting the times she had come to my aid.

The female peregrine sat on my right arm, glaring at the world. Before I could stop Soot, she glided over, landing with a thud, almost knocking me over. While I struggled for my balance, she climbed up my left arm to my shoulder, looking for her reward. Finally, she settled, sitting atop my head and leaning forward, peering down into my eyes. Even with a tight grip on the peregrine's jesses, I struggled to keep her from attacking Soot. I must have seemed very silly with a raven perched upon my head, as some people laughed and some gasped.

Encouraged, Da went on, leaving me to sort out my bird problem. "Folks, have ye ever seen something like this, a raven bonding with a lass. A falcon tolerating a raven." I could hear the grin in his voice as he continued. "A lass with a raven hat." The crowd laughed again. "My Nell can tame anything."

Ugh. Marketing strategy or not, as though this silliness weren't enough to embarrass me, I saw Jonathan watching from the sidelines.

Soot jumped back to my free arm and hopped from foot to foot, demanding her treat. The falcon finally had enough, bated, and screeched out her indignation at the invader.

A family with three or four children pushed forward to see, but too close.

With a bird on either arm, I was hampered and too slow to restrain Soot. The raven dipped down and grabbed a bun away from a small lass, quickly choking it down before I could intervene. Ruckus ensued, Soot laughed, the peregrine screeched again, and the child's outraged howl brought more people crowding in to see what was going on. Da expanded his patter to embrace the circumstances. "Aye, my friends, here's a bird with a devilish nature. Brazen, unabashedly brazen, stealing food from a wee lass, I've seen it snatch a morsel away from a hawk three times his size. It's brave and stealthy and devilish. In fact"—Da's voice lowered— "it gambles." One man in the crowd scoffed. Da held out his open hands. "'Tis true. The raven has an eye for coin. 'Tis more than just a bird. 'Tis a match for many a gambling man."

"So show us, Nat," someone called.

Da nodded. "Be pleased tae let ye in on its secrets, my friend, but it keeps them under its—feathers, so tae speak. But..." Da grinned. "Perhaps, just perhaps, we can arrange fer ye tae see what none other has seen. This raven's as cannie as any gambler. It follows in the footsteps of the rakes of London.

"But this afternoon, we'll be giving ye a show ye willnae see in four counties, a demonstration of skill and expertise with hawks and falcons. That's nae just me spouting hot air; my wee lass here will show ye what ye can do with a well-trained hunting bird."

"But about the raven; how does that bird gamble?"

Da didn't hesitate. "Ah, aye, the raven. Like I said, this isn't just any raven. This raven can outguess any of ye in a fair game of chance."

A large group of people bunched around, asking when.

"Come back same time tomorrow for a show that ye will be telling your lads and lassies aboot fer years tae come. Ye will see what a clever lass with a clever raven can dae."

After they cleared out, Da studied Soot, who appeared deep in raven thought, watching a child carrying a sausage across the way. "So, Nell, what think ye? Can we dae a show with yer bird here? One that will draw people tae our booth and demonstrate yer training skills. If they see ye can train a raven, they're likely tae believe our hawks are trained as well."

"She nae trained, Da. She only does what she wants, never what I want her to."

"But 'tis the trick. Have her dae as she will. Work it through, lass. Make her think it's all her idea." He held up a bit of string and a small hunk of sausage from his lunch.

"Create a small show of what she likes to dae. I'll run the patter. Ye just make it seem like she is following your lead."

I nodded uncertainly. "I'll try, Da."

Amusement danced in his eyes. "And Nell. How aboot we nae tell yer Ma aboot this? I'm not certain she'd think kindly about our little ruse."

Will returned, bearing news about dancers in the square. Da put the finishing licks of work on our booth before turning to him. "Will, how aboot we ask Ian tae watch our booth again fer a dance set or two? Maybe I can get some work playing for a rich merchant." He laughed at himself then. "Ah, ye both ken I want a wee bit of time tae enjoy music.

"Nell, soon as yer birds are settled, gan check out the Shaws' hawks. I'd like tae ken what they're offering this year."

I walked around, checking the other birds. They weren't any competition; they still had on blinders, so only half-trained. Soot flew down to a pole nearby. I had gotten into the habit of talking to her. "Probably doped up to appear gentle. Look, Soot, on the ground below them are loose mules, a sure sign of dropsy."

I noticed the telltale glisten on their tail feathers. Grease. They'd greased their feathers to make them shiny. Those folks knew nothing about caring for hawks. A dab of grease could make them look alert, though it wouldn't last. It could make them sick if you weren't careful. Our hawks were young and healthy—no better-trained birds around for miles.

A troop of belled and beribboned border dancers bounded into the lane. Their blackened faces and gaudy rag coats made them seem bigger than they were as they brandished sticks in pretend warlike whoops. I followed them down the way, trying to conjure myself as the wife of a merchant and failed. I nibbled on a hangnail that threatened to become a nuisance while images of me fancy dressed and seated on a velvet settee flashed inside my head. Nay, that couldn't be. I wouldn't be able to breathe without the wind in my hair and grass beneath my feet.

My path veered north to where the musicians gathered at the fair's center. A country dance was in full swing in the open circle. Da sat on a log, playing for the dancers. His second fiddle rested nearby. Two other musicians joined in. I noticed their fiddles and recognized Da's work. At Da's insistence, I accompanied them for a single reel. As I left, a fancy-hatted man approached, examining one of Da's fiddles.

I left, thinking of Da and Will and how we were going to manage. It appeared some better. And, though I wouldn't confess—Jonathan still crowded my thoughts, and what he had said about his grand. Which is probably how I got turned around and so far from our booth.

I smelled them before I passed—they must have been hanging out at the tanners, with its stink of urine. Four locals passing the day with talk. Angus and Derwin hailed me, and I walked over. The Wilson's boy, Harvey, looked me up and down, evaluating me like a heifer for sale at this fair. I was annoyed. I thought we had resolved this at my house.

Keeping the irritation from my voice, I smiled, nodding to those I knew. "Hey, Angus, Derwin, good to see ye."

Angus continued staring at me a little too long before speaking. "So has yer Da decided yet?"

"Decided what?"

He grunted in my direction. "Which of us yer to marry."

I frowned. "I'm in nae hurry to wed."

Angus frowned, but Harvey spoke before Angus could line up his handful of words.

"I got a bit of money put aside to get a wife. I'm thinking of offering soon on one that I'm going to court." He gave me a wink.

"Good for ye. I'm sure you'll find someone to suit." I was trying to be nice.

Angus smiled like he knew something I didn't. It didn't sit right in that blank face of his. I didn't like it one bit. "Me too. I've seen what's available. While it may be a little feisty now, if it comes with some gold, I'm willing to train it." He looked me up and down again. Harvey and Derwin hooted and laughed, like he'd said something clever.

Harvey pointed a finger towards me. "Be careful, we aw ken she's a mite feral."

"Sod off!" I glared at him, my nose getting quite out of joint with their needling.

It was harder to ignore their smirks and looks, and I wished I hadn't left Will behind. I was about to change the subject when I noticed Angus's green shirt with a badly mended patch. My head shot up, and I stared straight at him.

"What happened to your shirt, Angus? Got a tear in it, did ye?" I hissed.

His sullen eyes turned to me. "Must have got caught on a thicket thorn when we were out hunting."

I felt heat rise in my chest. He'd been one that tried to kidnap me. I knew it. "Did ye mess with something ye couldnae handle?"

"Oh, I could handle it well enough. It got lucky. We ken where it beds down. It's only a matter of time."

All their eyes rested on me now. A pack of wolves circling prey, but I was too mad to back down.

I spoke with bravado and no real ability to back it up. "Better make sure ye dinnae fall into a hornet's nest. Sometimes a wee animal can pack a wallop."

They whispered between each other, loud enough for me to hear—words that concerned bedding. Things they shouldn't have said. They glanced at one another and snickered.

A few people watched, but no one seemed eager to intervene. I felt myself flush, not with embarrassment, but with fury. My mouth opened again, and words come out—ones that Mam would have washed my mouth out for if she'd heard me. My hands balled into fists, tightened ready to throw a punch. I was trying to decide who to hit first. I was beyond figuring the odds of winning.

Jonathan silently appeared at my side. "There you are. I couldn't find you where we agreed to meet." I felt so twitchy, he was lucky I didn't clock him by accident.

I spit a good one their way before retreating down the dirt path with Jonathan, my back tense as I listened to the laughter behind me. Jonathan kept a light hand on my shoulder as I kept wanting to turn back and get the last word in—or fist.

"Were you looking for me?"

"No—Yes," he grinned. "You're hard to miss. Voices carry and not many lasses can curse like that."

I ducked my head, mortified that he had heard and that I had spit before him. What must he think?

"You seemed like you needed an excuse to leave Angus and his pals. I worried that there might be a fight."

I turned toward him. "Ye worried about me?"

"Not for you, I worried for them. I thought you might inflict harm on Angus. Harold's arm still shows the bruise you gave him."

"Oh, aye." I winced.

We came to another alleyway. A woman, her wrist crawling with bracelets, called over to us. "Buy your lass a bracelet, lad."

My cheeks flamed.

Jonathan raised a questioning eyebrow in my direction. I shook my head. I was not his lass, or was I?

"I'm in your debt again." I frowned, thinking about how many times he'd come to my aid in the last handful of weeks.

He grinned. "There's no debt between us. We're friends, remember? Besides, you've never needed much rescuing, though I find it impossible not to offer."

I grinned back.

Jonathan watched some beribboned acrobats. "Sounds like Harvey and Angus are seeking a bride."

I snorted and shrugged.

He grinned at me. "Sounds like you're not particularly taken with either."

I slanted a look at him, and he grinned again.

"Nope, nae them," I said. "But I promised Mam I'd keep my mind open to marriage."

"And is it?"

I sighed and shrugged my shoulders. "You saw those lads."

We strolled a little while longer.

"Why the sudden hurry to wed?"

"Mam's worried about my future. Times are hard, Da's hurting. He's fretting about Mam and the baby and money."

We stopped at a hastily put-up fence to admire a tinker's booth. Jonathan hopped over and waited for me to do the same. "Does this mean you are planning on marrying soon?"

I kicked at a rock on the ground.

"Seems like I dinnae have much of a choice. I can either make bundles of money with my hawks or I can marry well. Seeing the volunteers for my hand, I'd better get busy working hawks."

I glanced over at him. "You must think me such a lass."

He grinned. "Only in a good way." Then he went on, suddenly serious. "Don't you want to marry? You don't sound eager."

I sighed. "It's not..." I stopped, then blundered on, as I often did around Jonathan. "Eventually, everyone does." I tried not to glance over at him as I spoke.

Over everything, weaving into the wind and the noise, I heard Roselyn, like so many times before:

Rose, Rose, Rose, Rose

Will I ever see thee wed?

She stopped abruptly. Maybe the wind turned.

I was so startled by her voice again that my next words came out faster and harsher than I meant to. All my upset spilling out like grain pouring into a trough. "It's just that I dinnae want to be relegated to breeding and housework. I want to train hawks."

"And the husband? No interest?"

I blushed. "Don't be silly, of course I'm interested. But nae with someone like Harvey, Bill Bledsoe, or Angus Simpsin. If ye were a lass, would ye want to marry them?"

He laughed. "I see what you mean."

Jonathan stared off into the distance like he was seeing something. "What if that were possible?" he persisted.

"What?"

"That you could marry and still work hawks? What if?"

I looked up, hopeful, then shook my head. "Nae lass can. I've never seen anyone do that."

He reached over, placing his fingers a seed's width from my hand. "With the right person, it might be possible. I've always wanted to start my own rookery."

My heart sounded like the inside of a drum. A red flush crawled back up my cheeks. I was sure my freckles must be standing out. Here it was again. Could he be serious? I thought that he might be.

I ducked my head and changed the subject before I made a total dolt of myself. "Want to come with me to check on the Simpsins' bull?"

His one eyebrow shot up, and a wry smile crossed his face. "Sure. You thinking of breeding your cow to it?"

I whispered in his ear. "I'm thinking it might be stolen, and I'm thinking it's Will's."

Chapter

35

Both of us hunkered down. A black bull lounged within a knocked together shed. I knelt inches from Jonathan. His breath brushed my hair, little exhalations that warmed my face as we crouched there. His shoulder touched mine and I leaned into it, knowing that I shouldn't.

I left that comfort and squeezed beneath the railings. A second later Jonathan crept beside me. I took a vinegar-soaked cloth and rubbed it against the bull's rump. Jonathan stood at his head making calming noises. "Easy fellow, easy."

It came away black with dye.

Before we could leave, voices sounded from outside the shed.

We backed into the dark still holding the cloth.

"Well, now what?" he whispered.

I whispered back, "There's no magistrate within a five day's ride. Even if we were certain it was Will's bull…"

"Which we kind of are…" he said.

The door to the shed slammed closed and it was shadowy and quiet. Too quiet. Somehow, this felt different with him there. Different from all the other times Jonathan had been with me. Jonathan rearranged his legs to a more comfortable position. "Nell."

"Yes." Bollocks. My voice shook like a girl's.

"I realize that this isn't the most romantic spot for a proposal, but it's hard to get you alone and quiet."

I couldnae breathe.

His hand skimmed mine and stopped. "So will you, Nell?" He cupped my hand, my palm grimy with bull dirt, black dye, and who knew what else. Slowly, he raised it to his lips. "If we married, we could raise beautiful hawks together." His eyes questioned me. "And maybe a child or two." There was the lightest touch of my palm against his lips. Knees apart, we both sat and stared at the other. "What is your answer, Nell?"

"But I'm nae a Lady. What would our families say?"

"Nell, I want you, I love you. My grandmother approves. Your dad approves. It's just you who need to approve. So, will you?"

My head nodded up and down of its own volition. And he grinned. I leaned in and gave him a kiss. You might not think a bullpen could be romantic, but sitting with my love in the shadowy dark, with his warm body near mine, was more exciting than watching my first hawk soar. We tarried for one more kiss and then another. Arms and legs entwined, clothes loosened and bodies touched. Who knows what might have happened on that straw-covered floor if we weren't brought to our senses by a steady plop, plop, plop of bull dung a few feet from us?

"Well, now what?" I whispered against his chest. "Who do we tell?"

"About us or about the bull?"

I gave him a tickle. He retaliated. We ended up breathless, arms and legs entangled. After a few more lingering kisses, we forced our bodies apart and crawled out.

After yet another kiss or three, Jonathan headed to town to tell his family, and me, to Da and my hawks. Floating on air, I trotted back.

By the time I returned to our booth, everything was in chaos. And my news spun from my mind.

Our hawks had been poisoned. A heavy oil coating had been slathered on their feathers.

Da spoke as he dusted my goshawk with flour. "Someone must have been watching, as someone was nearby all day." He peered at my face. "'Tain't as bad as it seems. Will came back early from playing fer the dance. Only three were oiled. I'm guessing we can save them."

But we couldn't sell birds in this condition.

Will hurried back, carrying three feed sacks, a hole cut for the head. We carefully stuck each hawk in and gently shook the sack. Then Da filled a basin three fingers full of warm water and some mild soap garnered from one of the fair booths. He gently soaped our birds and handed them off one by one to Will, who rinsed them with clear water. I toweled them off and set them on their post to sun dry.

After half an afternoon's work, Da let air seep out of his lungs. "Let's wait 'til tomorrow, and if they aren't better, we may hae tae repeat this cleaning."

Though I managed to hide the tears that initially burst from my eyes, I knew I wasn't the only one devastated. Da's face showed he had aged five years and Will—Will looked like he had months ago, sad and lost.

It always seemed to happen. We'd have a dandelion puff of hope and watch it blow away with the least breeze. A will-of-a-wisp that couldn't catch its first breath before being whisked away by some disaster or another. And here we were again.

Da hunched on his heels, his head down. We were wiped, everything we had worked for destroyed. Only two of my hawks remained unharmed, both of my peregrines.

Da lifted his head. A spark glistened in his eyes. "Will, find the fair manager. Ask around. Someone must have seen someone hanging aboot here." Will left, his body bent like he carried a ten-stone burden.

My Da turned to me then. "Nell, get the raven ready."

His eyes landed on Soot, a glint in his eyes. "We have a change of plans. Put away yer tears and anger. We're going tae use yer raven's shell game tae recoup our money."

I pulled myself together and gussied myself up a tad for Da. He climbed atop a wooden stand, talking it up as people passed by our booth, like he was delivering a speech from a city stage. If you didn't know him, you wouldn't have guessed that our year's work had trickled away.

***

Soot and I stared at one another. She was suspicious, as were all ravens. She looked down from her high perch, twisting her head at me. She knew I had treats, and she also knew something was up. Twenty people gathered round to see us perform. I hoped she wouldn't make me look an eejit. Soot had no interest in pleasing me, and who knew how she would react with this many folks standing about?

Da's voice carried over the fairgrounds. His sing-song patter drew a crowd. More people stopped, peering over one another, to see what the fuss was about. This was our last chance to earn some coin.

His patter made it seem like Soot and I were a team. But Soot wasn't eager to team up with anyone. She was out for herself first, and her stomach second. I came a distant third in her reckoning of who to please.

"Now. What ye see up there is a raven, a common scavenger, but watch. My lass can train anything, even a raven." Da pointed to Soot sitting high on a pole where a jaunty banner flapped in the gentle breeze.

Da nodded at me.

I held my breath, hoping for the best. Carefully, so she would see, I cupped a piece of sausage in my palm. Soot noticed at once; she missed no opportunity to get easy food. She glanced from me to the crowd and back to the sausage, as if considering.

Please, please, don't get all raven-ish on me now. Soot ruffled her feathers, shaking them out like she was settling down for the evening. People snickered. I gritted my teeth. Once more, I held up my hand. Soot turned her head away, and I despaired. She wasn't going to come, probably too large a crowd, too many other things to notice. Some people wandered away, but then Soot lifted off and flew to my arm. The crowd gasped, and I breathed again. I quickly snapped a tether on her left leg.

Da started up his patter again. "Here we gan, folks. Like I said, 'tis an ordinary raven. Nae gimmicks, nae hidden secrets."

Only a short time ago, we'd figured out a plan. Please let it work! Two small wire cages were set upon a tall box with three cords dangling out. In the first cage were three of our doves, two short sticks, and a longer one. Da held the sausage between his thumb and index finger. As Soot watched, he placed it inside the other cage. Soot looked away and then back. She dearly wanted it. And it was only accessible by knocking it out with the long stick.

Soot hopped up and down, quorking, trying to get free. I held her tether tight, knowing what she would do.

He waved his hand toward a young lass with long hair, encouraging her to come forward.

I pulled out a wooden whistle, holding it low.

"So, lass, tell us yer name?"

"Shona."

"'Tis a fine name. Nell, would ye ask yer raven what she thinks about her name?"

I wiggled my whistle so only Soot could see it. Soot wobbled her head back and forth and then let out a long whistle. The crowd was delighted.

"Now, Shona, could ye help my lass here?" She nodded and smiled at me like I was a goddess.

"Ye can see there are three cords there. Only one will release the birds inside. Shona, would ye hold up the cords so everyone can see?"

Soot knew how to figure this out. She'd unlatched many of my cages before, much to my dismay.

Shona lifted each string up, one after the other. Two of the strings attached to the door but did nothing. One hooked onto a lever, and if pulled, would open the cage.

"Good. Now, Nell, set yer bird down. Let's see if it can puzzle it out."

I gave her some line on the tether. Soot strode over to the cage, inspecting each as only a raven could do, nodding and bobbing her head. Finally, she decided on the cord, grabbed it and stepped back, tugging until the latch opened. Three doves flew out the other side, trailing different colored ribbons. The crowd oo-ed and ah-ed, watching the birds rise above us. Soot ignored it all. She only had eyes for the stick that would let her get the sausage. I tugged her back, and she snapped at me.

"Now, my friends, it's gotten closer tae figuring this out. See, there are three sticks to choose from. With only one, can it reach the sausage. What dae ye think will happen if we release the raven?"

"It will peck at the cage door," someone hollered.

"Fly away," someone in the front yelled. The group laughed.

"Maybe yer right, Hamish. And maybe it's a clever bird. How aboot we take a show of hands? Who thinks the bird won't figure this out?"

Da's voice softened, cajoling. "Any of ye willing to put a penny on yer choice, my friends? Or should we just call this a warm-up fer the real thing?"

He waved a hand at the crowd. "Hamish, still here, are ye? Yer a daring sort. What say ye?"

Hamish rocked on his heels, his thumbs resting on his trousers. "Maebe, maebe not. 'Tis my penny." The crowd laughed.

Da tried again. "Any of ye brave and cannie enough? 'Tis only a penny."

A brawny kilted man pushed forward, reaching into his sporran. "Aye, I have a penny that says the bird cannae do it."

"Then come closer so ye can ken we're nae cheating. Nell, let the raven go."

Soot marched over, lowered her head, and studied each stick. She grabbed the longest stick, galloped over to the cage, and whacked the sausage out. It disappeared with a single gobble. The crowd roared with laughter. More people crowded around.

Da handed Shona down from the stand to her awaiting Mom.

Da had the crowd in his pocket. "And here, folks, we have the real thing ye've come tae see. A game of chance for adults." Da held up three walnut shells and another piece of dried meat. "I'll place the shells down in a line. And, Hamish, ye be an honest man, why dinnae ye come up and keep this game on the up and up?"

Several people pushed him forward onto the raised platform where Da stood.

"Now tell me, is there anything unique about these shells— some hidden compartment or some way of hiding anything else inside? Now check carefully. I'll nae have it said that we cheat. Maeve, ye want to join him and check them over too?" A short woman with a merry face joined Hamish. They turned over the shells, conferring to each other as they did. Hamish ran his fingers across each shell like there might be a trap door.

"Nay, they are as you said, plain nut shells."

"Would ye place them down in front of ye, please?

"Good, and here is some dried meat. One of ye put it under a shell." Soot hunched like she would leap forward. I held her tight.

"Nell, now before ye step up here and start the game, roll yer sleeves up tae yer elbows so our gentle folk won't think ye hae anything hidden."

At the applause, I chanced to look out into the crowd. One thing caught my eyes. A glimpse of a green shirt with a patch over the arm. Angus again.

I couldn't react, not in the middle of Da's show. But Soot saw him also and screamed out a challenge, "Thief!" She tried to fly, only the restraint kept her on my arm.

The crowd applauded, and I remembered where I was. Soot, easily distracted as always, bobbed up and down. Angus disappeared into the crowd. I had to let go of giving chase. We needed this money. I calmed myself, promising I would deal with him later.

Da continued his patter, making a big show of putting down the three shells, showing all that nothing was inside any of the three. Soot watched, flexing her wings, twitching her back muscles like a boxer preparing to go into the ring.

More people gathered round, and Da was busy collecting coin from the audience, a half-penny a piece. I'd better make this good.

"Thought you gave up gambling when you married, Nat," a voice called out.

"What's that city wife of yours going to say about this?" another hollered, as a stream of tobacco hit the dirt. Laughter started up amongst a group of men.

Da's eyes clouded over. "Maura's a wise woman. She would say that her daughter can dae anything she puts her mind tae, and I would agree." Da lifted his head, looking straight out at the men laughing. "And folks, she's going tae put her mind tae this."

"So, does that mean you're willing to put real money on it?"

Da was quiet, studying me, knowing we didn't have money to lose.

Will left off working on the hawks and place a silver coin on the bench. "It's not gambling if there is no chance of losing."

Jonathan emerged from within the crowd with another coin. "I'll put money on Nell."

Da smiled. "Well, folks, ye heard them. Ye willing tae match their bets? Thomas, how about you? Are ye willing tae put some money on this? Ye dinnae believe a mere raven and a wee lass could beat ye, dae ye?"

***

I danced around with joy as Da counted out our winnings. He beamed like it was his raven, as if he hadn't wanted her gone twenty times over. Of course, most folks wised up after our first couple of wins. The bettors dwindled quickly. Only three fool-hearty men thought they could out-think a raven. But the crowd stayed, watching the shells scoot round and round and Soot cavalierly toss off the shell and grab her booty. When it was over, I stood, blinking tears of joy from my face as I listened to the crowd cheer for a common raven. Our takings more than covered the cost of our discounted booth fees.

I couldn't wait to show Jonathan.

Chapter

36

People were packing up and heading home with a jingle of money in their pockets. Mothers called for their errant children. Some late-night reveler sang, and a bunch of people joined their voices with his.

I counted our take for the weekend. I'd sold our two remaining healthy birds, though not for what I had hoped. But a merchant from the town across the river had requested my services to retrain their falcons. A promise of paying work and my first solo job away from home. The most startling thing that happened was the contests. The Simpsins' bull, Will's bull, won best of the fair, and the Blair's mottled sow took second.

The surprise came when my raven, Soot, came in as best-trained animal. A tribute to my ability to train anything, the judges said. I floated on air from the praise. And it came with a smidgeon of prize money. I glanced around for Jonathan, hoping that he'd returned by now. He would be excited for me, pleased and happy.

Considering what had happened, what could have happened, this was a good fair. And thanks to Will's quick thinking, our remaining birds would live. Will was busy loading up the dray. As soon as we had a moment, I would tell him about the bull.

Da limped over like he was in shock. I grabbed his arm. "What's wrong? Is it Mam?"

He waved his hand toward a fancy-dressed man drinking a tankard of ale down the way. "He just gave me fifty ducats fer my ash violin." At my open-mouthed look, he continued. "And a written promise tae purchase ten more violins at the same price."

"Oh, Da!"

He looked happier than a retriever dog with a duck in its mouth. "Yer Ma is nae going to believe this." He gave me a hug. "Let's finish packing up and gan home, lass."

Before we even set foot on the path home, my brother Hal met us, bent over from running.

"The babe arrived. Aunt Bess says ye must come home now."

"What's wrong?"

"Naught that I know. Mam didn't want to worry ye..."

Da gazed around at our half-loaded dray, at me. His face went from joyous to concerned to stricken, as he thought about the fifteen miles he had to travel.

He was itching to be with Mam. Many people were leaving. Will checked our sick birds one more time, making sure they were well-watered. Da approached friends, asking if he could have a ride to get back to Ma sooner, but no one was heading to our side of the county.

Amidst all the rumble, mayhem, and kicked-up dust of a fair ending, Jonathan's grandmama rolled up in her carriage. "Mr. Pritchard, might I have a word with you?"

Da tipped his hat. "Beg pardon, but I hae tae get tae my wife. She's just birthed, and I need tae be at her side."

Grandmama took in the panic in his voice. "Let solve this. Here, join me. I'll get you back in a third of the time, and we can talk on the way."

Da looked at my brothers and me.

"Da, I'll be fine. Will and Hal are here. We'll be right behind you."

"Be careful, Nell. Stay close tae yer brothers."

"As close as a tick on a hound." Hal nodded, but Will must not have heard, as he didn't turn his head.

Da laughed. He closed the carriage door, and they drove off.

Will slipped away as Hal and I finished loading the dray, making sure all was tightly tied and well-balanced.

Everything was ready. Soot took off for a tall pine tree to investigate a squirrel's nest. I knew we wouldn't be on the road more than a mile before she winged her way with us.

A half hour passed, and Will still hadn't appeared. Though the fair was winding down, people fussed about, knocking down their booths, patting one another on the back, having one last pint of ale.

The afternoon shadows grew longer. Hal circled the dray again, checking for any imbalance. "If we don't leave anon, we won't make it back before full dark."

"You go on. I'll get Will, and we'll be right behind you."

Hal scanned the sun and our sick birds loaded on the dray. "Aye, we need to be moving."

I gave him a cheery wave and headed off to find my eldest brother.

Chapter

37

The moon eased itself over the horizon as I wandered about. The wind picked up a mite, blowing leaves and fair debris across the fast-emptying fields: tattered cloth streamers, a dirt-encrusted oatcake likely dropped by some luckless bairn, broken bits of twine that had held up gayly painted banners. A few folks bustled about, finishing packing, most having already trundled down the roads, and still no Will. No one had seen him since Da had left. The inside of my cheek was raw from my chewing at it. Will had been too still before; why, why hadn't I watched more carefully?

I took a quick side trip to check on the bull. Afar off, I spied Angus's bull tethered to a cart. Okay, not there. I would have to wait to deal with that.

As I wandered about the mud-caked heath, avoided patches of scratchy gorse, circled around the hillocks and a few clusters of trees, it came to me in a feeling of being punched. I knew exactly where Will was. Where I had planned to go also.

The Tower. But I didn't have the ring with me.

The breeze became a gust as I raced toward the road that led to the Tower, paying little attention to my surroundings. My hair worked loose from my carefully plaited braid, making it hard to see clearly. Every minute counted. I stumbled over a log, brushing away a sudden flurry of leaves that flew into my face. It would be full dark in two hours, and I wouldn't be easy on the road after that. I'd have to find a place to land and start up early morn.

Someone called my name.

***

When I think back, I can see my first mistake was separating from Hal. The second was taking it in my head to see if Angus's bull was still around, thinking Will might have guessed it was his. The third. Well, there's always a third, isn't there? That one probably explained the lump on my head.

My hands were rope-bound, and a rag covered my eyes, but I didn't need eyes to know it was Angus and his pals. I could smell them. The cart wobbled along, and every rut in the path marked my spine. As my head thumped repeatedly on the wooden slats, I got madder. This wasn't right. Every time I turned around, I got trapped by someone. It had to end.

I squirmed about, banging my head even harder on something as I tried to get loose.

"She awake?" Derwin asked.

Someone poked me with a stick, and I howled.

"Aye," Angus replied. "She's awake."

We stopped only for bodily functions. After some serious grousing, they deigned to untie my hands, though I had only the count of fifty to do my business behind a scraggly yew before they yanked the rope on my leg. I screamed like I was being killed in the hopes of more gentle treatment or that someone might hear me on this lonesome road. 'Twasn't to be. That's when they added the mouth gag.

As you might guess, I did not have a fun time.

I stewed, madder than I had been since Cam and Ben tossed my only ragdoll in the mud when I was six.

Since I couldn't see to track the moon and stars, the night felt achingly long. I had plenty of time to ponder my situation.

My family must have guessed where Will went. Everyone would be upset and concerned.

But with my disappearance, Da would be panicked, Mom distraught, my brothers worried. Two of the family were in trouble.

Jonathan might not find out for days unless he stopped by. My thoughts raced to what he would think, that I left for the tower, which I had planned—but I hadn't.

***

The next morning began when I had only just closed my eyes. Worn to a nub by my fretting and my attempts to get loose, I hadn't rested easy. The lads let me have my fifty seconds of privacy, handed me cold oatmeal, and tossed me back into the cart.

We thumped our way through another day. I was spitting mad and planning all sorts of revenge once I got loose.

High above, I heard a voice croak, "Resist." Soot! She had followed.

The cart pulled to a stop, and a voice called out, "There it is. We'll be rich."

Roselyn crooned to herself again. I feared that meant she had Will.

Rose, Rose, Rose, Rose
Will I ever see thee wed?

I heard the lads leap out and scuffle about. Someone crawled up on the cart, near my feet. "Not so sassy now, are you?" I kicked out. My foot connected with a body part that was soft and squishy. The cursing afterwards proved that it was Derwin. There weren't many people with that foul a tongue.

"Hey, where's the ladder?"

"She kicked me!"

"Deal with her after. We need to brace the ladder onto the Tower. Then we'll drag Nell over and get the gold." Harvey muttered threats to me before hopping off. There were scraping and thumps as they maneuvered something off the cart—their ladder, I guessed. It was hard to tell from inside the cart and blindfolded, but lots of grunting and groaning were involved.

From nearby came an urgent quorking. The whir of wings and a hard thump as the soft silk of feather brushed my hand. As Soot's scaly claws wrapped about my arm, I wriggled my hands, hoping she would undo the knot. She knew how to do this. She had unraveled this kind of problem before, first with the coneys, then the fruit basket.

Of course, only when it suited her.

Please, Soot, please. Don't go all raven-ish on me now. I could hear the boys struggling with the ladder. It wouldn't be long before they came back.

I rubbed my face against a bale of wool, and the rag slipped down from my eyes. Soot stared at me like she expected me to get up. I thunked my head down, exhausted, then wrestled with the rope again.

Roselyn's voice ratcheted louder, that insistent repetitious round that she sang.

I will marry at thy will, sire
At thy will.

Roselyn's croon hiccupped to a stop. Beyond, though not far, the boys argued; something wasn't right.

"What are you doi—?"

"Angus, stop. Listen to me, don't touch the..." I heard a slurping noise, and Harvey's voice came again. "Oh, my lord."

"Did you see that?"

There were more wet sucking sounds that didn't bode well for Harvey or Derwin.

Whatever their problems, and I was certain there were plenty if they were messing with Roslyn, I didn't have time to worry over them. I raised my hands up, focusing on encouraging Soot. She tossed shreds of twine hither and yon, examining each piece like it was a puzzle. And then, finally, my hands were free.

Of a sudden, Roselyn stopped her calling. I guess with three new victims, she was a mite distracted.

I rolled out of the wagon. But the Tower seemed totally different from months before. It was all wrong, like the ground beneath it had swallowed up foot after foot of the Tower. The window I had gazed out, the balcony I had hung over during those months, was no longer a long drop.

I so wished I had Bess's magic ring, but wishes wouldn't help now.

Soot and I kept our distance, not moving closer or farther, as we took in all the changes. The white walls were mottled with thick spiderlike webs. Roslyn's webs.

The ground grasped at my foot when I took a tentative step closer. It felt wet and squishy, bog-like. The thought came to me that she had enchanted the ground also, but with further checking, it was only wet, muddy ground. I grabbed a couple of wool pelts from the wagon and tossed them across as stepping stones to the Tower base.

A long ladder lay abandoned nearby, crude, but sturdy enough to hold weight. The Simpsin boys must have made it when planning this trip. The boys, as I might have guessed, were gone. They hadn't even had time to maneuver it up against the walls.

A short climb and I could be in, if Roselyn would let me and if she didn't grab me during the process. But I was Will's sister, and I supposed that Will might be inside now. She might not harm me. Lots of ifs. There was no turning back for me. I walked around the

Tower base, taking my time, checking for a place where I might enter unharmed.

Finally, I laid one of the pelts under the ladder to keep it from sinking and began my climb.

Chapter
38

I started up, not knowing who I might find—my brother, my captors, Roselyn, the wraiths—or no one.

After scrambling over the railing, I hopped down and walked inside. The invisible wall that long ago blocked my way no longer existed, but otherwise, the interior was much the same. The curtains remained ripped and torn from when I escaped. My braided rope lay limp, tied to the banister as I left it.

Across the room, Will knelt inside the panel. A shimmer of magic blanketed him as his mouth stretched in a soundless scream. My gut twisted like it contained a nest of vipers.

Sitting beside him, Roselyn wept. This mustn't match her dream of them together again.

As all my rational thoughts left me, I flung myself forward, screaming and pounding the wall. "Let him go! Let him go!" At each blow my fist stuck, sinking into the shimmer of the panel, and I had to drag it back.

Neither of them seemed affected. Roselyn didn't notice. Will remained locked inside his nightmare.

Sobbing uncontrollably, I crouched before the panel. I was back where I was two months ago; too late, and still no magic.

Roselyn's face registered confusion and distress. She knew something was wrong. Her unease caused a constant vibration in the tower. She had Will, but felt his pain and despair. Not the joy she had expected.

In the left of the panel, two lads stood knee deep in a pond, with bodies like herons. A frog sat on a lily pad at their feet. With human ears and his bulbous nose, the frog had to be Angus.

I did warn them.

I didn't care. I didn't. I needed to get my brother and Dulce freed. Nothing more.

But a single glance at the panel and I hesitated. So easy to enter, I had felt its pull from the moment I climbed over the balcony rail.

The Guardian watched me, his face painted in shades of mute horror.

I appealed to him. "Help me. Please. Make her let him go."

His eyes taking in the magnitude of the disaster before him, he remained silent.

I folded into a heap on the floor.

A great lethargy sank into my body, paralyzing my muscles, sifting down through my bones. Why was I resisting, anyway? Maybe I should go within the wall also, complete the picture in that last panel, let myself be absorbed. Maybe that was the way to rescue Will. Once within, I could force Roselyn to understand the pain she was causing.

My eyes drooped, half closed, and I leaned in nearer. I could lie beside that clear, tranquil pond. It appeared so welcoming, so restful. No more troubles, no worries, no…

Something dove, slapping against my side.

Soot.

Soot circled the room, flying low overhead before clamping her talons onto my shoulder. All the lethargy, all the desires to slip peacefully away, shattered and dissolved as she pecked at my ear.

As I backed away from the panel, my whole body shivered.

"Nell! Are you there?" A voice reached me from what sounded far away.

I shuddered, terrified at what almost happened.

Jonathan! He had found me. He'd noticed I was missing and followed.

"Dinnae come up here," I warned. "You'll be caught."

He spoke to someone outside then. There was a grunt and the sound of a body struggling up the ladder.

As he clamored over the railing, he muttered, "So you can take all the risk and no one else?"

I couldn't stop myself from rushing into his arms. "Jonathan!"

"It's all right," he soothed, patting me on the back.

"Nae, it isn't. She has Will now. We're trapped. She'll never let him go."

Dulce's voice yelled in my ear. "Resist."

Jonathan's long exhale told me he recognized his sister.

Inside the warmth of his embrace, he whispered over and over, "We're all getting out of here, all of us." His warm breath licked my neck until he leaned away from me and gave me a shake. "Nell, this isn't who you are. You don't give up. You're being gamed."

I glanced back at the panel. Roselyn was cradling Will, rocking back and forth, trying to comfort him.

The other wraiths spilled out of the walls. Moving out of Jonathan's embrace, I scanned the room, searching for anything that would help.

Then I heard the Guardian make the mistake of speaking. "This is heartrending. I wish I could undo all this."

My spine straightened as cold, burning fury rushed in.

"Ye can!" I railed at him, realization slamming against my

ribs. "Will did what ye said. Respected your wishes, stupid and mean as they were, and went off on that fool's quest. You've caused many lives to be damaged, including your own. Ye owe me. Ye owe Roselyn and Will and every person locked in this Tower."

He held his hands up in defeat. "There's nothing I can do. I've tried everything. You know that."

"Nae! There's one thing ye haven't done. Tell her. Tell Roselyn ye stole her letters, that Will never forgot her. Tell her. Tell Roselyn that she can marry whoever she will. That ye will bless their union. Tell her!" I screamed. "Otherwise, I will tear this Tower apart block by block. Starting with your mirror." I picked up a cello, wielding it like a bat.

Roselyn suddenly solidified. Her body paused its rocking.

The Guardian deflated as I spoke, his eyes flicking to Roslyn and back to me. "Roselyn will attack if you do this."

I took a breath. "Then I die, but so do ye." Everything seemed to gel into this one moment as I faced the individual responsible for all the heartbreak and misery of those trapped here. "Listen to me. I. Want. My. Brother. Back," I could barely speak for the great, racking sobs that caught in my throat. "And all the other lives locked in there. All of them. We're going to end this now. Forever."

He was shaking his head, even as I spoke. "Nell, you know nothing can break this mirror. You've tried before."

He was right.

"The only thing that ever affected her was my playing."

I breathed, suddenly aware of the answer. I dropped the cello, grabbed the fiddle, and started fingering the tune that had caused the ruckus before.

The Guardian pressed his hands against the mirror in panic. "Don't! Stop!"

The walls rattled, and the floor shivered.

Beside me, Jonathan pivoted slowly, watching the wraiths circle in closer with every passing moment. Dulce separated herself from the others, moving to stand with her brother, both hands outstretched to push the others back.

My Aunt Bess struggled over the balcony and clambered into the room. Her voluminous skirt tucked up in her waistband like someone from a foreign story tale. Her carefully coiffed do now fallen down her back.

The Guardian's gaze locked on her as she scrambled inside.

"Bess!" His words breathed out of him.

She drew herself upright, every inch the mannered woman, and addressed him like she knew he was here all along. "Hello, Edwin."

"Help me—stop her from causing this destruction."

"Her?" my aunt repeated, her eyes narrowing as she regarded him. "You mean your daughter, Roselyn, don't you? Not Nell, my brave, bonny niece. Nell's here to set things right."

He blinked, caught off guard. "No, you don't understand. I'm working on it. I can fix this."

She snorted. "Like you fixed Roselyn's romance. Like our parents fixed our romance. Was that for the best, Edwin?" She examined her fingers as if she were seeing them for the first time. Then her voice dropped almost to a whisper as she glanced up to look him in the eyes. "You never came for me. You said you would, remember?" Slowly, she pulled off the pewter ring, reading aloud the inscription inside. "'Our magic is forever.'" She snorted again. "That didn't last long, did it?"

She glanced toward me and then, with a flick of her wrist, tossed the ring at the mirror.

Though the walls creaked and the windows shook, the Guardian couldn't seem to break his gaze away from her.

Bess dismissed him then with a turn of her head. She scanned the room, noting the fiddle and the various instruments, before resting her gaze on the harp. "So, Edwin, you kept that, did you?" Not awaiting an answer, she sat in the chair, straddling the harp.

"Nell, may I join you?"

With a slight, grateful smile, I nodded.

She rang her fingers across the strings, listening. "What do you wish to play?"

"Her song. The song she and Will wrote. Their love song."

Bess gentled the harp pillar into her arms and nodded.

I started with an eight-bar intro, something to warm up my fingers and give Bess time to learn the tune. Edwin, the Guardian, hadn't moved since Bess last spoke to him and thrown his ring. As we played, his image seemed to grow less gauzy and transparent.

The floor trembled and shifted beneath our feet, but we both continued. Jonathan stood behind me, his hand resting lightly on my waist. Oh, there were a few missed notes here and there and a handful of the harp strings might use more tuning, but neither of us quit.

Once I played, I didn't bother glancing toward the Guardian. But then I heard him speaking. His voice came soft and hesitant. "I only wanted what was best for you. Always. All my choices were to help you." It increased in volume. "You deserved riches and a good life." I was unsure who he was speaking to, Roslyn or Bess.

His gaze traveled from Bess to me to include all those caught in this drama and, as he did, it seemed a dawning awareness traveled across his countenance.

Tears fell as the words finally spilled out. "He always loved you, Roselyn. I confess it. I sent him on a fool's quest and destroyed his letters." His voice rose again until he was screaming. "You knew, didn't you? That's why you've done this. To punish me." He was sobbing now, but strung between the notes we played, I could hear a soft refrain coming from within the wall. It was Roselyn, singing the old traditional round that she crooned when I inhabited the tower. Over and over she sang it. I put down my fiddle and joined her, coming in two measures after her and singing it as a round, as it was meant to be.

Rose, Rose, Rose, Rose,
Will I ever see thee wed?
I will marry at thy will, sire, at thy will.

Bess added her alto, two measures after, lightly strumming the harp strings so it didn't overwhelm the vocals.

By the second time around, a fourth voice joined in, Edwin's, but the words now changed.

Rose, Rose, Rose, Rose
Will I ever see thee wed?
You may marry at your will, lass, at your will.

Both Bess and I dropped our vocals out, continuing to support the tune as Edwin sang the new refrain repeatedly. His voice rose as he emphasized the new lines. Roselyn continued, her eyes closed. She finished the last line of the round, her eyes still shut but her body turned toward the mirror where her father still sang.

I heard her whisper, "I will marry at thy will, sire."

The emotion in Edwin's voice called even to me. "No, Roselyn. You may marry *at your will* or not at all."

She stopped then, her head tilting as though she heard him for the first time.

Her eyes flickered, but they didn't open. The walls vibrated again, and this time, stone fell from the ceiling. Bess and I jumped up and dashed for the balcony. Jonathan took shelter at the bedpost.

But Soot stayed. Against the wall, a thin lock of Roselyn's golden hair dangled out of the panel. Soot took hold and tugged. Roselyn's eyes snapped open, startled.

Edwin's voice softened, pleading this time. "I was wrong, Roselyn. Let them go, Roselyn. I beg you. Do what you will to me, but don't punish all these others." The mirror cracked. I ducked.

When next I looked up, I noticed the spider first. He spit out of the wall and scuttled across the floor in a rush. A sparrow or two flittered out and lay stunned on the rich gold and rose carpet. And then two more, Dulce and a young man. Jonathan raced to help them up, pulling them away from the walls. Others tumbling out, falling onto the push carpet until the only couple remaining inside the panels were Roselyn and Will.

Finally, with tears streaming down her face, Roselyn released Will and turned from us. I ran to help, but he gently pushed me back.

The Guardian remained centered in his mirror, staring at the freed people. Only my kidnappers remained within the walls, still posed as waterfowl and frog.

Will stood directly before Roselyn. I grabbed his shirt to pull him away again, but Jonathan whispered in my ear, "Let him try."

I frowned but let him lead me a couple of steps away.

Will said nothing for a long time. If I didn't know better, I would have thought he fell asleep. His head remained lowered, as if deep in thought. He leaned toward his lost lover and breathed. Finally, he lifted his head and spoke. "You have a choice, you know."

Roselyn flinched but didn't turn around.

"I'm here waiting. Not everyone gets a second chance—but sometimes, some places, a door opens, and you can stretch forth and redo."

Roselyn turned her head, her eyes still closed, but her shoulders now leaned against the wall.

"I heard you. I heard your thoughts. Yes, you hurt people, many people, but you're not the only one who's made a mistake. Look around you. Just in this room, see all the mistakes that have been made.

"Forgiveness is what we are all about, isn't it, my love? That's what we are here for, that's what life is about. So now, Rose, forgive your father for wanting the best for you. Forgive me for leaving. Forgive yourself for fighting for what you wanted in the only way you thought you could. All of us have tried and failed. But we're trying again. You can, too. Open your eyes. We're standing here. We're all waiting for you. I'm waiting for you."

She didn't seem to hear him or move. But then, with a creak and a crash, the mirror broke. Out stumbled Edwin: Roselyn's father, my Guardian of the tower, Bess's first beau. It was complicated.

Will didn't flinch. He leaned forward more, his forehead touched the wall, his palm pressed flat against the seventh panel. "Come, Rose, reach for me. Take my hand. Just step out."

I could see the tears spilling down her face now. She opened her eyes, then covered her face with both hands and shook her head.

Will kept talking. "You've proved that you are strong. Strong enough to hold true. Strong enough to forgive your father. Now you can let it go. Forgive yourself. It is time to take what is offered, what you fought for. What we both worked so hard for. Come, Rose, turn to me. Take your life back—and complete mine."

Slowly, her hand came up and joined Will's, both pressed flat against the other. Her fingers lifted and intertwined with Will's, slipping outside the walls into the room. He drew her with him, first her hand and then an arm. As her face emerged, he kissed her cheek and then her forehead. She lifted her lips to his. They kissed so long that I glanced away, embarrassed. Finally, Will gathered her into his arms. She sobbed, her face hidden against his chest, her arms wrapped about his neck.

And Will—he looked like a man with the whole world in his arms.

Epilogue

It was only a tinned mirror, but one so like his prison of seven years that he took an involuntary step back.

He steadied himself before contemplating the weathered man reflected. A man fast approaching fifty—a man reshaped by time and pain, no longer so proud that he couldn't acknowledge how hard that adjustment had been.

"There you are. We're almost ready to begin. Do I look suitable?" His betrothed wrapped her arms about his waist, reminding him of how fortunate he truly was.

He basked in the feeling of her arms. After years distanced from life, never would he be indifferent to a loved one's touch.

"Ah, Bess." He kissed her palm and held her out before him. Her eyes shone, and her hair flowed in waves down her back. "You are glorious!"

So much had changed and so much was the same since his time locked within the Tower's mirror. The grass appeared greener, the sky bluer. In the distance he could hear a bull bellowing. Will's bull, recovered, with the stolen money, after the thieves returned from the Tower, subdued but grateful to be back into their own bodies.

That ordeal was over.

All that he had demanded for Roselyn was not worth a farthing to her. The only thing she wanted was her love, Will. And today was the glorious joining of the two who had waited so long, never giving up on the other.

The wedding was as it should be: family, friends, music, and much joy. Roslyn kept it simple with garlands of wildflowers as decorations. He proudly walked her down the aisle to her waiting groom. Will said not a word but placed a simple pewter ring on her hand right as he said, "I do."

Guests brought food to share, and musicians came from across the county. Music flowed from the moment Roselyn walked down the aisle on his arm straight through to the party after, where she and Will danced to a new piece they both wrote, the "Journey's End" reel. And during it all, Will was dressed in a smile of such joy that even Nell's brother, Cam, danced with a local lass.

Though Nat Prichard still favored his leg, he and his wife, Maura, danced a couple of sets. At least when someone held Maurine, their new baby girl.

He thought he caught a bevy of hostile glares, but no one spoke ill to him or Roslyn. Many apologies and a liberal distribution of coin had bought silence, if not forgiveness.

He glanced over to see Nell dancing with Jonathan, her hair untidy, a cheek smudged, work boots peeking out from under her dress, her face aglow.

She was the last Lady of the Tower, and from his perspective, the very best.

The
End

Acknowledgements

This book has been pinged around for so many years and is finally coming out. So many people have critiqued various iterations of it and helped shape it into a cohesive read. Thank you, all of you.

Susan Rush Rouch
Val Hobbs
Jeanine Kitchel
Kitty Donohoe
Mara Bushansky
Ted Chiles
Sia Morhardt
Robin Winter
Jeremy Gold
Kimberly Troutte
Sherrie Petersen
Christine Casey Logsdon
Angela Borda
Mari Talkin
Rachel Quisel
Lori Walker
Nancy Tubbs
Pauline Brand Nelson

And a big thank you for the ones who helped to package and gussy it up.

Kevin Barry, line editing
Angela Borda, Book design
Laura-Susan Thomas, Cover design

Gwen has a BA in psychology, and training in computer information systems; for most of her life she worked as a systems analyst. When she wasn't at work, she danced on English folk dance teams. She also loves doing ceramics and stained glass as well as baking and gardening. She's gone to Outward Bound, jumped horses and solo backpacked. She has a Golden Retriever and is married to a soil ecologist at UCSB.

Visit her at www.gwendandridge.com.

Gwen is the author of:

> The Stone Lions
> The Jinn's Jest
> The Dragons' Chosen
> The Lady of the Tower